CAGED WARRIOR

ALSO BY ALAN LAWRENCE SITOMER

The Hoopster

A Teacher's Guide—The Hoopster

Hip-Hop Poetry and the Classics

Hip-Hop High School

Homeboyz

The Secret Story of Sonia Rodriguez

Nerd Girls—The Rise of the Dorkasaurus

Nerd Girls—A Catastrophe of Nerdish Proportions

BY ALAN LAWRENCE SITOMER

HYPERION

LOS ANGELES • NEW YORK

For information address Hyperion, 125 West End Avenue,
New York, New York 10023.

Printed in the United States of America
First Edition
10 9 8 7 6 5 4 3 2 1
G475-5664-5-14046

ISBN 978-1-4231-7124-9

Library of Congress Cataloging-in-Publication Data to come

Reinforced binding

Visit www.hyperionteens.com

SUSTAINABLE FORESTRY INITIATIVE   Certified Sourcing
www.sfiprogram.org
SFI-00993

THIS LABEL APPLIES TO TEXT STOCK

Dedicated to Quinn, the fighter & Sienna, the strong—
Always believe in yourselves, girls.

With special appreciation for Wendy Lefkon,
pound-4-pound the best! And Al Zuckerman,
a man who believes in me—and brings out
the best in me—like no other.

Plus, a deep, loving kiss for my inimitable Tray, a giant
hug for my bro Roberto, and the biggest fist bump I've got
for G-Money. (And a li'l shout-out for the GaGa's, too.)

"THE FIRST THING I THINK ABOUT
WHEN THE CAGE CLOSES IS,
I HOPE GOD
FORGIVES ME FOR
WHAT I'M ABOUT
TO DO."

—Anonymous

ONE

Some people call it human cockfighting. They're wrong. Mixed martial arts is a sport. A bloody sport. A violent sport. A sport filled with pain and hurt and injury. But inside the cage, the sport is filled with something else, too.

It's filled with truth. See, it doesn't matter who you are—life is a fight. A ferocious one. Being an MMA warrior simply reveals what you're made of on the inside.

Me, who'm I? Name's McCutcheon Daniels. Soon as I was born my father started calling me M.D.

As in, "If you get in the cage with my son, you're gonna need an M.D."

When I was nine I pulled off my first flying arm bar and snapped an opponent's elbow at the joint like a crispy fried chicken wing. The sickening *crack* made a middle-aged lady in the front row faint.

Must be her first time at the Sat Nite Fights, I thought as she collapsed to the ground. People in the audience just stepped over her to collect their winnings on the bets they had placed. Everyone knows there ain't no love lost between gladiators in a Detroit cage fight. Apparently, there ain't no love lost cageside, neither.

At the age of eleven, I used a gator roll to land my first anaconda choke hold and took out an opponent three years older than me, a kid who up until that point had never lost a match. He tapped out before I could rip his shoulder off.

I always respect the tap. Not like some fighters who add a bit of stank to their work after an enemy has already surrendered. Without honor, a fighter has nothing.

At fourteen my skills really began to develop. In one fight I choose to go sprawl-'n'-brawl against a fool who had at least twenty pounds on me. Dude wanted get all down and dirty and grapple. Woulda been smart for him, too. What was dumb was he hadn't spent more time working on his stand-up striking defense because he ended up eating a Muay Thai knee smash to the center of his face.

I needed six stitches to seal me back up after the broken chunks of his teeth were removed from my knee. Later that night, I sat on a stained sink in a dirty gray locker room that smelled like sweat, mold, and lingering farts while a white-haired old man with a white beard injected a three-inch hypodermic needle into the cartilage below my kneecap. Wanted to make sure I didn't get tetanus or something. I watched as the silver syringe slowly pierced my skin, disappeared into my flesh, and shot streams of liquid fire up my nerve endings.

I didn't flinch. Not even wince. Instead, all I could think

about was one thing, one question that looped over and over in my mind.

Did doing all this make me a savage?

Without my shirt on, my abs carved from granite, bubbly scars from where torn flesh had healed, blood trickling from my cut, swollen knuckles, I know I looked vicious. And glistening "where-exactly-is-he-from?" skin color only added to that sense, too. My dad's half black, half Asian. My mom's half Hispanic, part Anglo, and got some Brazilian mixed as well. They say that's where I get my bright white eyes, tanned-by-tropical–island-sun skin, and long, thick eyelashes. Basically, I'm a street mutt.

But was I an animal?

No.

Way I see it, a man's gotta do what a man's gotta do. Even if I am barely sixteen. Nope, it ain't pretty, but fact is if I don't win, Gem don't eat.

For me, the math doesn't get more simple than that. I mean what kind of older brother lets his five-year-old kid sis go hungry?

"You're lettin' this punk overhook you," my father shouted, a chunk of white spit flying out of his mouth as he yelled at me. His bubbly spew landed on my shoulder and though we both saw it, we both ignored it, too. "Don't go for the clinch. That's what he's expecting. When he comes in to tie you up, hammer this bitch with an elbow smash, look for a throat strike, and if it ain't there, spin around, bury your heel in his kidney, and make him piss blood for a week. Got me?"

"Yes, sir."

"Good," he roared. "Then end this fucking thing! Remember, leverage, leverage, leverage."

Some kids have dads who raise them to be golfers. Others, quarterbacks. Still others to play tennis or soccer or baseball. I was raised to cage fight. Ever since I was three, my dad schooled me to brawl. Taught me to grapple, box, ground-and-pound, strike while standing up, and submit an opponent while lying down. From Sambo to Brazilian jiu-jitsu, Greco-Roman wrestling to Aikido, joint locks to pin holds to pressure-point manipulation, I'm an assassin in the art of hurt. My father wants me to do more than just defeat my opponents; he wants me to destroy them.

"It's how champions are made," he tells me. "And one day, you will be world champion."

"Yes, sir."

How do I feel about all this? Fact is, I don't really give much thought to those kinds of questions. Feelings are luxuries when there's a growl in your family's stomach.

The bell rang to begin Round Two. I rose from my stool and headed back out onto the dance floor, my body a weapon poised to strike.

It used to be that there were no rounds at all in underground cage fighting. When I first started out, opponents just went toe-to-toe gladiator-style until there was only one warrior left standing. However, a few years ago the Priests recognized that having seven-minute rounds followed by ninety-second battle breaks created more action.

And more bloodshed and more dynamite exchanges

4

and more destruction, too. Therefore, since those were the things that paying people loved to see, those were the things that paying people got. The only thing that really matters to the Priests anyway is the money. As the Mafia-style organization in charge of underworld cage fighting, the Priests of the Street were a criminal crew who understood that happy customers would also be returning customers. Sanctioned fights could be seen at home on TV. Raw, underage, gloveless, savage wars could only be seen live.

Funny, but bootleg recordings of the Sat Nite Fights and piracy wasn't really a problem for the Priests, either. Not at all. Ever. Anyone who had the balls to try to secretly film our cage battles to post on the Internet would discover the pleasure of tire irons shattering their shinbones or brass knuckles tickling their jaws. Too much money was being made on the weekend war circuit. And too much attention on the underground battles could jeopardize the other streams of black-market cash the Priests were raking in from their wide variety of extensive criminal enterprises.

Essentially, as a gang, the Priests had their fingers in all kind of pies, so they made sure every fan in attendance was aware of the rule: the No Cell Phone policy would be strictly enforced and violators would get no second chances.

The break in the rounds, however, didn't just give fighters a small rest to collect their thoughts, regain their wind, and rethink their strategy; they gave the peeps in the crowd more of an opportunity to place extra side-bets, too. Broke people just love to gamble, and the more money in the air, the more energy, excitement, and juice. In this country, it's all about the cash. Anyone who tells you different ain't never slept in the hallway of an unheated apartment building before.

I rose from my stool and took a moment to center myself, to slow down my breath and focus on the mission at hand. The night's fight was going down in an abandoned middle school on the outskirts of D-town. Rusted pipes hung from the ceiling, broken school desks lay tossed in a corner, a makeshift cage made out of jagged steel fencing that looked as if it had just been stolen from a nearby construction site had been set up in the center of what was once a gymnasium. When I first started brawling, I'd be lucky if there were thirty people watching. Tonight, there musta been three hundred.

Success has a way of doing that for a fighter's career.

"Do like I say now, M.D. It's killa instinct time." My father's eyes were wild, his pupils the size of dimes and pitch black. "The cheese comes from a KO in Round Two. You know the old man's flying naked tonight, right?"

"Yes, sir."

"Good," he told me. "Then do your thing."

Sure, I coulda finished this dude in Round One, but there was more money to be made through betting if I prolonged it a bit, dragged things out for my dad and made the match look closer than it really was. Of course, to do this cost me a few blows to the face—one shot to the ear really spanked me good—but that was the price to be paid so we could get those extra dollar bills.

But now that Round Two was here, it was time to end

the evening. The sooner, the better, as far as my father was concerned. That's 'cause my dad hadn't just placed a bet on me to win by K.O. in the second; he'd placed a bet he couldn't cover. That's what he meant by flying naked. If I didn't finish my opponent in the next four hundred and twenty seconds, chances were excellent that my father would be leaving the venue in a neck brace.

Maybe even a body bag.

Nobody messed with the Priests.

No pressure, right?

At the crack of the bell, the seventeen-year-old Samoan at the other end of the cage charged forward. His arms were the size of legs, his legs were the size of tractor tires, and after one round of rolling around with him in the center of the battle box, I could tell that size was his strength.

But size wasn't ever what determined who won or lost inside the steel coop. Size could be neutralized. With technique. For the Samoan, his mass came at the expense of speed and agility, so I began Round Two with a flurry of quick jabs from the outside.

One-two, in-'n'-out, one-two, almost classically boxing. He lunged at me. I slipped his clumsy swipe, ducked, and countered, *one-two,* tagging him good. Then I pump-faked a jab and fired off a blistering leg kick that landed with a *Boom!* Some spectators don't think sidekicks to an opponent's thigh really do all that much in a cage fight. Obviously, they've never been smashed in the leg with a baseball bat.

Hands up, in-'n'-out, rat-a-tat-tat, more jabs. One of

the Samoan's eyes began to twitch. He raised his hands to better protect the side of his head I'd been peppering, clearly favoring his left.

And favoring his left meant he'd become vulnerable on his right. I saw my opportunity.

"Let him in," my dad ordered with a *What-are-you-doing?* scream. "Let the little whore in!" Nervous that this match might head to Round Three if I didn't hurry up and take the big fella out, my father belted out instructions. Sure, by striking from the outside I'd whittle my opponent down—however, as my dad well knew, a victory against a kid this size was only gonna come through grappling, not striking, because on the ground is where I'd either choke him out or get him to submit. Stinging jabs weren't going to bring down an oak tree.

By my mental calculations about three and a half minutes remained in the round. "Let him the hell in!" my father screamed; and so, despite the fact that I had planned to take a different path to victory, I did as my father ordered and let him in.

It was a mistake. I recognized it immediately. The Samoan lumbered forward looking to clinch, and I missed with an elbow smash, barely grazing the right side of his cheek. A moment later he capitalized and locked me in a bear hug. His adrenaline flowing, his rage boiling, the laws of physics behind him, he began to squeeze. The Samoan's plan was simple: crush me like a disease-carrying bug crawling across a white kitchen counter. The fight had swung his way.

Well, at least for a moment it did.

My counterattack began with a heel smash. It landed on the top of his right foot like a jackhammer, but still he squeezed, seeking to restrict my air intake. However, with all the roadwork I do, I knew I could count on my oxygen supply to last me for a good long while, so I allowed him to trade me squeezes for smashes, and I dropped my heel again. Then a third time. My fourth fell on his foot like an anvil, and I could feel the metatarsal bones on the top of his right foot break underneath the force of my blow.

The pain caused him to loosen his grip. I quickly slithered out of the Samoan's smothering grasp and shot an exploding uppercut to the base of his chin. It didn't land flush, but my spinning back punch to his unprotected midsection hammered him with the force of a cannon.

It was my best shot of the fight.

And it was the last shot I'd need.

It's one thing to see an opponent fall from a knockout strike to the head. Seeing an opponent fall from a knockout strike to the midsection, however, was something else entirely. It meant I'd gone beyond a mere body blow; I'd damaged an organ.

The Samoan fell to a knee and wheezed. Blood began to fill his mouth, red liquid covering his white teeth like a bottle of spilled shiny cherry paint. Internal bleeding, I thought, a classic sign. Like a cougar I was on him, my knees pinned to his shoulders, my fists and elbows ready to rain down a hurricane of terror on his unprotected face.

The crowd cheered wildly, thirsty for destruction. Fear

came to the Samoan's eyes. I narrowed my gaze into daggers of heartless ice and paused. He'd get one opportunity to tap.

He took it. Fight over.

I stood, turned, and walked back to my corner victorious, the fans in attendance exploding with cheers.

Bam! My father smashed me across my face.

"Finish your opponent!"

A warm stream of salty liquid began to trickle from my lip.

"You always finish your opponent."

I didn't respond.

"And don't you dare look at me like that," he commanded. "I know, you're thinking, 'Hell, I won, didn't I?' Well, you ain't never gonna be a world champion without the killa instinct."

Willie the Weasel, a skinny guy with a crooked teeth and a poorly inked neck tattoo of a pair of unevenly drawn dice, interrupted. A low ranking Priest, Weasel served as the go-between who set up all our fights. He talked too much, he talked too fast, and despite all the words that came out of his mouth, a person never knew which ones were true and which ones were bullshit.

"Good fight, kid, good fight. Here's your cheese." Weasel extended his arm to hand me a manila envelope. Tonight's fight was a fifty plus three, meaning that each fighter got fifty bucks for showing up with the winning fighter taking home an additional three thousand dollars for putting a W in the win column.

The loser, aside from a broken body, got nothing more than half a Benjamin.

My dad snatched the envelope and peered suspiciously inside.

"It's all there, Demon. It's all there."

Didn't matter a gob of spit what Weasel claimed, my dad wasn't letting anyone go anywhere until he counted every last nickel.

"G'head then, check it," Weasel offered. "G'head."

"Damn right I will," my dad said.

"Priests always pay, Demon. Everyone knows that. Priests always pay."

My father licked his thumb and began working his way through the chunky green stack of paper. "Just shut the hell up a second, Weeze. I'm doin' mathematics."

Weasel, shrugging off my dad, turned to me and smiled. "Whadda fight, kid. Tremendous fight. No time at all, you'll be drawing big-digit paydays. I can see it now, pay-per-view."

I wiped my face with a towel and thought about how I'd just inched a step closer to prime time. All the major warriors in MMA started like this, as backyard brawlers with something to prove. After all, the recipe to arrive as a big-name, big-money draw wasn't some sort of secret; everyone knew what needed to be done to make it to the top. A fighter had to post a string of W's, earn a local rep, become a dependable payday for the gamblers, and then score a couple of breakout wins against a few high-quality opponents—the more violent the victories, the better.

That was the path to follow. That was the path I was on.

Like every sport, a nonstop hunger existed in MMA for new stars. Once I was old enough to fight legally, there's no doubt I'd get my chance under the bright lights on the big stage. I just knew it in my bones. Spill enough enemy blood, and the word gets out.

Yep, one day I'd be a main attraction.

Satisfied with what he'd been handed, my father turned to Weasel.

"All right, you good."

"I told ya. Did I tell ya? I told ya."

"Shut the hell up, Weasel."

My dad began sifting through the thick wad of cash. I watched as he rifled past the hundreds, past the fifties, and down to the bottom of the pile where the smaller bills were buried.

"For you," he said handing me four twenties and two tens. Slowly, I took the money.

"Thanks."

"Don't thank me, son," my father said wiping his nose on his sleeve. I watched as he took the winnings, folded the bills in half and stuffed the fat stack of cash into his pocket. "I love you."

TWO

I'm the only son of the great Damien "Demon" Daniels, a welterweight boxer who boasted a professional record of 28–2 on the day that I was born.

By the time I turned three, his record had dropped to 28–9. After losing to the world famous Sugar Ray Leonard in his first and only title fight, my dad got TKO'd in the fifth by Thomas "the Hitman" Hearns as he was trying to climb his way back up the rankings. Then, a year later, my father got "knocked the hell out" by Marvelous Marvin Hagler and suddenly, the great Damien Demon Daniels was no longer great.

Soon my father was being used by boxing promoters as a tune-up fighter for the next round of up-and-comers. Seven straight losses after his title shot had taken him from "potential world champion" to "tomato can."

And drug addict. And alcoholic. And gambling, whore-chasing, thieving, lying parolee who was constantly on probation. After his last ugly Round Two defeat at the hands of a no-name Cuban, it wasn't long before my father was out of boxing entirely. However, a new sport was starting to emerge, and Demon Daniels, being a tough guy, felt cocky about being able to knock the block off of any ol' street fighter that dared to get in the ring with a "genuine" professional.

Way my father saw it, there'd be no chance a non-boxer could ever compete with a fighter who possessed hand speed, an ability to throw crisp combinations, and knock-out power in both hands.

Ten thousand dollars for the taking if my dad could claim victory in this thing no one had yet really heard of called "The Octagon." An undersized, not-too-muscular fighter who'd stopped through Detroit while on tour across America to raise awareness for his Brazilian family's specialized style of no-holds-barred street fighting would be his opponent.

Royce Gracie, now famous but back then a total unknown, took my dad to the ground twenty-two seconds into their fight, and my father, witnessing his first ever wristlock—from the wrong end of witnessing a wristlock—tapped out before he'd lasted even a full minute.

That was his introduction to mixed martial arts.

That was also when he decided that I was going to be a world champion. But not as a boxer as he'd originally planned. Instead, he'd breed me to one day dominate the exploding new world of MMA superfighting.

All this makes me a second-generation warrior, the first of my kind. Gen number one of MMA fighters were all crossovers who came from other schools of combat. Some came from wrestling; some, like my dad, from boxing;

some from karate; and a lot—the best—came from BJJ, Brazilian jiu-jitsu.

But I'm a purebred. I come from MMA, a sport where all the styles are meshed, mashed, and blended together in order to create the ultimate fighting machine. Conquest in the cage is what I've been trained to achieve since the crib, and my father swears to anyone who will listen that by the time my career is over no one will have ever done it better.

Pound for pound, I will be the best.

"Who's tough?"

"I'm tough."

"How tough?"

"So tough."

"And why are we tough?" I asked, a look of steely determination in my gaze.

Gemma, wearing her hair in pigtails, looked at me with big, soft eyes. "'Cause that's the way we get out," she answered, a large, dimpled smile on her face.

"Gimme a kiss," I said. My sister pecked me on the cheek. "Didya have a good day?"

"Awesome!" she answered with a skip in her step. Gemma slipped her tiny hand into the soft part of my palm and we began walking down the sidewalk, home from Harriet Tubman Elementary School. "First, we talked about caterpillars and how they form cocoons so they can turn into butterflies. Then, we got to color all these shapes but I already knew all the names of the shapes so Miss Marsha let me trace the letters of the alphabet but I already knew that, too. Can we get a chinchilla?"

"What?"

"Miss Marsha says that on Friday we're going to pet chinchillas and I've never petted a chinchilla before," Gemma continued without missing a beat. I swear my sister's tongue is like a long-distance runner that never breaks stride. "I petted a goat once. And a salamander, too. Salamanders are cold-blooded but they have moist skin. I wonder what the chinchilla's name is. Can we get one?"

"Nope."

"Pleeeeease, Doc?"

"Nope," I answered. "Entirely a nope."

"Not fair," Gemma replied.

My sister is the only person on the planet who gets to call me Doc. Actually, my mom used to call me that, too. Before she ran out on us a few years ago, that is. When she left, she took the only source of steady income, the only source of steady meals, the only source of steady smiles, faith, or warmth under our roof, too.

Just one day: *Poof!* Diss-a-peeeer'd.

"But why can't we get a chinchilla, Doc? Chinchillas are nice and they're furry and they sometimes eat lettuce and I could even brush its teeth."

"Doesn't kindergarten do hamsters anymore?"

"Now that I think of it, we need two chinchillas and a carton of ice cream. Remember that time I had a scoop of mint chip, but there weren't enough chips so I had to complain and the owner gave me a whole bunch of extra rainbow sprinkles because he ran out of chocolate chips?

I bet chinchillas would like mint chip ice cream even if it didn't have rainbow sprinkles."

I'm not sure Gemma's mouth stopped motoring the entire twenty-minute walk home down East Seven Mile, a street famous in D-town for all the wrong reasons. Gemma's hand never left mine, not for a second. Too many monsters in the area to even count.

We crossed the highway overpass, turned left at the graffiti-covered Dumpster, and entered through the ragged entryway of our four-story redbrick building. The apartment door, once white, hadn't been painted in years. A short walk down stale-smelling halls and up two flights of moldy, chipped wooden stairs brought us to apartment 303A.

Home sweet home it wasn't.

I unlocked the door, and we got straight to business, unzipping our coats, tossing off our backpacks, falling immediately into our regular routine of snack, homework, and then artwork for her while I prepared supper. After dinner, it would be bath, book, brush teeth, prayers, kiss, bed for Gem. Monday through Friday, five days a week, this was the plan, and the plan was never in question.

I love routines. I'm a creature of routines. Routines are our way out of living a life that we share with roaches, rats, addicts, and gunfire. Fact is, when you sleep sideways on a sheetless couch and shower in a bathroom where the hot water hardly gets warm on days when it snows—and in the Motor City, it snows a lot—while your younger sister wears used sneakers that you buy at Goodwill and doesn't even own a bicycle, well...that'll make a person hard in all the places a heart is supposed to be soft.

But the right routine can give us wings to fly away. Fly to a place from which we ain't never coming back. This is why I train like an animal. Discipline is the gasoline of dreams.

Sacrifice? Don't mind it. Pain? As they say in the gym, pain is just weakness leaving the body. Add it all up and my weekday schedule is 100 percent locked. I rise at four a.m. to do two hours worth of roadwork, and then I'm at Loco'z every day after school for three more hours, sparring, working on technique, sweating, and bleeding.

Without fail.

At night from nine to ten thirty p.m. I hit the kettlebell I keep underneath the kitchen table, alternating muscle group sets depending on the day of the week or the injury I'm nursing. After a late-night shower, my own prayers to a God I'm not even sure is really listening, and ice packs if needed, it's off to bed by eleven, 'cause less than five hours' sleep doesn't give my body enough time to rest and rebuild itself for training the next day.

Everything in my world revolves around routine. Including Gemma. Every day I am the one who drops her off at school, and every day I am the one who picks her up.

Without fail.

And every day we begin and end with the same words.

"Who's tough?"

"I'm tough."

"How tough?"

"So tough."

"And why are we tough?"

"'Cause that's the way we get out," she answers.

"Gimme a kiss," I tell her. And she does.

These words are the music of our relationship.

Sad as it may sound, Gemma's not just my only sibling; she's my only friend. At my high school, well...I'm kind of a loner. Probably 'cause not that many other kids my age have to deal with all the stuff I have to deal with, being the main money earner, doing all the shopping, cooking, and so on. Me and them, I guess we just don't really relate.

"Hey, Gem, I got an idea."

"Chinchilla?"

"No," I said. "But, well...whaddya say we go get pizza?"

She stopped, her purple crayon frozen mid-stroke.

"You're gonna eat pizza?" Gemma knew all too well that proteins and vegetables with limited carbs and virtually no starches were entirely my thing. One of the guys I used to train with down at Loco'z, a black belt named Ripper, introduced me to this concept called Paleolithic eating last year. Basically, it's where a fighter eats like a caveman.

"If it wasn't available to them, it's not available to you," he told me. "In a hunter-gatherer's world you need a hunter-gatherer's diet."

I tried it. Within two weeks I saw how my body was stronger and recovered faster from both training and beatings. Gemma knows I not only work out like a crazy person, but I eat like one, too.

But she's a good kid. A really good kid, and sometimes when I look around and see that she's got no mom and can't play in the streets once the sun starts to set and doesn't ever complain about all the toys she doesn't have, well...she deserves a break now and then, don't she?

"O' course, I love pizza," I told her. "Matter of fact, I'm gonna have pepperoni on it, too."

"Oh yeah," she answered, her eyes lighting up like a Christmas tree. "Well, I'm gonna have a chocolate sundae afterward with hot fudge."

"Oh really?" I said. "Then I'm gonna have a piece of cheesecake, a slice so big it'll take me two forks just to get one bite."

"I'm getting a side of meatballs," Gemma hollered. Meatballs in red spaghetti sauce was her favorite food of all time.

"I'm having root beer."

"Me, too!" she replied.

I closed the kitchen cupboard from which I had been about to snag a frying pan. "Grab your jacket. Race you to the door."

"Can we also play some of those games, Doc?" Gemma softly asked, a hopeful look in her eye.

"You mean, play that machine in the restaurant where you stick dollar bills inside and try to grab a teddy bear but that clutcher thing is rigged so that no matter how many bucks you feed into the stupid game, no one ever wins?"

"Uh-huh," she said, nodding her head up and down.

I smiled. "Sure. And tonight," I added as I reached for

my secret can of protein powder where I kept all my extra savings after I bought the groceries and the medicine and stuff like that, "tonight I am scoring you a teddy."

"YAY!" she shouted.

My hand fumbled upward for my secret cash stash. From my tippy-toes, I pulled the can off the shelf. It felt light. I opened the plastic top and looked inside.

My eyes dropped. Immediately, Gemma knew what had happened.

When you live with an addict, it always happened. Had happened a hundred thousand times before. Slowly, quietly, I set the can back on the shelf. Gemma began to unzip her jacket.

Without a complaint or even a comment, Gem returned to the kitchen table and picked up her purple crayon. Me, I trudged over to the fridge in order to see what could be rustled up.

Coupla eggs, a few tomatoes, some noodles in butter for Gemma. That'd be our dinner.

Wouldn't be the first time, neither.

Deep breath, dude. Deep breath.

Later that night I dimmed the light in Gemma's room. Sure, I may have been sleeping on a torn-up couch in the living room of a crappy two-bedroom, one-bath apartment, but damn if she would.

"Who's tough?"

"I'm tough."

"How tough?"

"So tough."

"And why are we tough?" I asked. Her head lying softly on the pillow, she looked up at me with big, tender eyes.

"'Cause that's the way we get out."

A lump formed in my throat.

Not wanting her to see me weak and vulnerable I lowered my eyes and double-checked her blanket to make sure she was tucked in good and warm.

"Gimme a kiss," I said.

She did, and I closed the light.

THREE

I 've never been inside any of those schools that you see on TV shows, the kind where most of the students are white, all of 'em got up-to-date books, and the hallways look like they just got a fresh coat of paint over the summer. My school is on Fenkell Avenue.

You wanna see real D-town, come to Fenkell. Not at night of course. Tourists don't last long on Fenkell once the sun sets. But come during the day, and the streets'll be filled with all sorts of local sights: noontime hookers, broken-down, toothless old men who limp, liquor store after liquor store after liquor store. The streets of Fenkell are bad.

Fenkell High is worse.

Some of my classes have sixty-two kids in 'em. With one teacher. That's when the teacher even shows up. And forget about subs; they just jam us into the cafeteria and have us wait and do nothing whenever one of our "dedicated staff members" calls in sick. Place is a complete joke. A person can buy drugs, shoot dice, score a weapon, or fence stolen property in the halls. And speaking of the halls, the things that some of our lady scholars do in the hidden corners, well…I swear, the place is more fit for demolition than education.

What's extra sad is that Fenkell High is being used as a combination middle and high school these days because Fenkell Middle was closed by the Department of Health. Asbestos in the ceiling tiles or something like that. The potential for youngsters to be poisoned forced them to cram fifty-six hundred students under one roof as a "temporary" solution.

This is the third year of that "temporary" solution. Some schools have trophy cases and vending machines on campus; Fenkell has dried bloodstains and used condoms.

A loud bell signaling the end of fourth period pierced the air like a state-of-emergency alert. "Hey, McCutcheon, stick around a sec, would ya?"

Mr. Freedman was always asking me to "stick around a sec." Guy's my science teacher, the type of person who never misses a day of work. Man could have the flu, the mumps, tuberculosis, plus be missing a kidney, and he'd still show up the next day with a lesson plan on the inner workings of organic molecules.

"You see this?" he asked holding out a sheet of paper. Mr. Freedman, the gray hairs starting to outnumber the black ones around his temple area, always wore a tie, always wore a watch, and always looked a person straight in the eye when he spoke to them.

"So?"

"A perfect score on your anatomy quiz," he said. "A hundred percent."

"Lucky, I guess."

"Lucky?" he asked.

I shrugged. "Yeah, well, you know ..."

Fact is, anatomy's easy for me. Like I coulda smoked that quiz if there were three times as many questions. After all, I'd been studying the human body for years. Part of the job description in my line of work and all.

"Not luck, son. Brains." Mr. Freedman used the eraser end of his pencil to point at my forehead. "Tell me," he asked moving the eraser downward to point at my swollen cheek. "What happened to your face?"

"Skateboarding."

"Skateboarding?"

"Uh-huh. Skateboarding," I said.

He nodded, scanning me top to bottom. There was a long silence as he measured me up.

"You coming to the auditorium tonight?"

I squinted, the twisted look on my face answering the question for me. *Like why would I be coming to the auditorium tonight?*

"It's the charter school lottery," he explained. "Nine neighborhood schools, 1,673 balls, just four slots. They pull 'em bingo style."

"I'm not much for bingo," I said.

"Those bingo balls, they represent an opportunity, son." Mr. Freedman put his hand on my shoulder in a caring, fatherly way. "You know, not much officially counts for college in terms of academic records until you get to your sophomore year, but if you post solid grades in eleventh and do it again in twelfth, especially at one of these charter schools, you're looking at a way out."

"I already got plans for my way out."

"What's that, skateboarding?" he asked, as if he knew something more than he was letting on. Very few folks, students or teachers, hadn't heard about the growing reputation of the cage-fighting kid from Fenkell High who was born with a gift for breaking holds, breaking bones, and then breaking other fighters' wills.

"Somethin' like that," I said in a low-key manner.

Truth is, I had to give Mr. Freedman his props. The man really did care about the kids at our school. A student can always tell when a teacher is faking it. He wasn't. Mr. Freedman was one of those guys who went way beyond the paycheck to try to be a role model, to try to be a sort of good citizen in a place gone insane. Despite the fact that so many of his so-called students often acted more like they were in a zoo instead of in a classroom, Mr. Freedman always did his best to teach them and reach them.

Even when they didn't give a flying flip about being taught.

But I guess he saw something in me. Like some sorta potential. That's why, I imagine, he was always asking me if I "had a sec." Can't really fault a man for that. Plus, I'm the kind of person who prides myself on being polite and prepared for class with my homework and stuff, anyway. Way I see it, discipline in the cage can only be obtained by having discipline outside of it as well, and though this may sound weird, I'm one of those students who never once got into a fight at school.

Not once.

Of course, having a rep like I do doesn't hurt. People up and down the halls know, *Don't mess with Bam Bam*, a nickname I picked up somewhere along the way. But the thing is, I like rules. I like respecting them, too. I guess I just prefer it when things are orderly and go the way they're supposed to. Me, I like neat. I like clean. I like it when A + B = C. Chaos, mess, it bothers me. Come to my kitchen and every pot has its place. Every pan, every fork, every plate, too. No, we don't got much, but what we do have is in its proper spot. If I get homework, I do homework, simple as that. Of course, I also know that this doesn't give Gem any excuses for slacking off, either. I mean, if I'm gonna cross all my t's and dot all my i's, then damn straight she's gonna do the same; but the reality is I just can't sleep good unless I know I have properly handled all of my business each and every day.

That's just who I am.

I glanced at the clock on the wall above Mr. Freedman's desk. It was broken, stuck on 8:18. I didn't know if that was a.m. or p.m., but it didn't matter. After science class every day I had to be somewhere.

"Can I go now?" I asked.

"You should come tonight," Mr. Freedman said, as if he was actually dropping a hint. "I got a feeling you could get lucky."

Lucky? I ain't never been that. Besides, my dad hadn't even filled out any of the forms. Far as I knew, I wasn't even eligible for the stupid charter school lottery.

"Sure," I said as I flipped my hoodie over my head. "See you there."

I made my way toward the dark-green classroom door that led out into the hallway, knowing that there wasn't no chance I'd be watching bingo being played later that night.

And I felt pretty sure Mr. Freedman knew this, too.

What I would be doing by twelve thirty that afternoon, however, was mashing down at Loco'z Mixed Martial Arts Center, a place where the mats smelled, the bathrooms did, too, and the fighters were hard, scarred, take-no-prisoners cage warriors.

"I'm gonna snap that sucker's bones like a fat girl snaps a chocolate-covered pretzel!"

BOOM! Officer Klowner pounded the heavy bag.

"Dude's so soft, people blow their nose into his armpit fat!"

BOOM! BOOM! Klowner struck again.

"Boy wanna get in the cage with me, he's either blind, stupid, or can't afford cable TV!"

Klowner spun with a roundhouse kick, and *KA-BOOM!* It sounded like a mortar round had just been detonated inside the gym.

At six feet four, two hundred forty pounds, David "Officer" Klowner was a former U.S. Marine who'd gone past the black belt level in Tsien Tao Chinese Kempo to earn a red belt. Leg strikes were his specialty, the kind that could knock down a house. His motto: All business in the cage, all smiles outside of it.

"Remember when I KO'd that dude in Philly and the ref asked him where he was and the boy said, 'Uh...Vegas?' Man, I done knocked that fool clear across three time zones." Klowner machine-gunned the heavy bag, sweat flying off his body like bullets. "Ain't nobody want a taste of this honey bear."

"Hey, K-K-K-Klowner, when's your m-m-m-manager think you're g-g-g-gonna get a title fight?" Nate-Neck asked with a stutter.

Nate-Neck was called Nate-Neck because, well...he didn't have one; his shoulders went straight to his ears and his head sat directly on top of his traps—no neck. Once upon a time he'd been a championship wrestler at the University of Iowa. Now, at twenty-seven years old, his world was all MMA, twenty-four hours a day, seven days a week.

Not exactly what anyone would call a pretty man to start with, Nate-Neck had a nose that zigzagged like a bad country road and a case of cauliflower ear that would scare off young children. Of course, cauliflower ear is a warrior's badge of honor, especially to a wrestler. A person can only get it from spending so much time with their head being rubbed into the surface of the mat that their earlobe becomes permanently disfigured. Nate-Neck's left ear looked like a chew toy for a pit bull—swollen, deformed, inflamed, a permanent rash—and while no, cauliflower ear won't do much to attract the ladies, to an opposing MMA warrior, it shows a kind of toughness that can't be bought with a mere tattoo. Ink you can pay for; cauliflower ear has to be earned with blood, pain, and years of hurt.

Standing five-foot-eight and two hundred and five pounds, with a chin made of cement, Nate-Neck was as tough to dent as a bank vault. Kids used to tease him for the way he "s-s-s-stuttered" when he was in elementary school. No one teases him these days unless they have a very good health insurance plan and a high threshold for bodily pain.

"Got three weeks till my next undercard," Klowner answered. "And once I obliterate Jersey 'J.J.' Jenkins, it's only a matter of time before I get a shot at the belt." Every fighter in the gym basically had one reason for living: win the belt. And when it came to talk about belts, not even Klowner clowned around.

"Yo, M.D., w-w-w-what's up, kid?"

"Hey, Nate," I said as I approached the lion's den.

"Up for s-s-s-some crucifix work today?" he asked.

"If you have time," I said as I set down my gym bag.

"And I got you lined up for hip sweeps later, right?" Klowner added. "Plus clinches."

"Yes, please, if that's okay."

Klowner repeated my words in a squeaky high, girlish sounding voice. "Yes, please, if that's okay." He smiled ear-to-ear. "Kid, you gotta be the most polite badass I've ever met."

I grinned. "Lemme just sweep up the locker room before we get rolling, okay?"

"And make sure my towels are fluffed!" Klowner called out. *BOOM!* He smashed the heavy bag with a high roundhouse that landed like thunder. "My foot is like a sleeping pill with toes. Who wants some?"

Lord help the man who took one of Klowner's kicks to the head.

I'd started coming to Loco'z when I was nothing but a squirt, so young that lifting a bag of wet towels used to push me to my limits. That's when a few of the fighters started taking me under their wings, showing me some moves, that kind of thing. Being that my dad, Demon, used to box with Loco under the same trainer, a semifamous guy named Palm Tree Taylor from way back in the day, I became the young'un who got to hang around when Loco opened his own place, sort of the pet puppy of the gym, who never had to pay dues or anything to use the facilities.

But puppies grow up. Nowadays, after I make myself useful by helping to clean the place (even though Loco never asks, but it's only right) I mash with the big boys.

And they don't spare me one bit from the hurt of training. At least once a week I walk out of Loco'z with less blood in my body than I walked into the place with. Most MMA fighters who are serious about their craft know exactly what I'm talking about, too. In this sport even the winners get hurt.

Hurt bad.

"M-m-m-mouthpiece?" Nate-Neck asked, making sure I had my safety gear.

"Check," I said flashing my teeth.

"Cup?"

I banged my balls with my knuckles. Nate listened for

the *click* sound of the hard plastic. Once or twice I'd been known to try to sneak through without all my gear. It's not that I don't believe in being safe, it's just that, well... I can't always afford everything.

"Go s-s-s-start your circuit," Nate said, noticing that my dad, the guy who is supposed to be my manager, my cornerman, and my trainer, wasn't—as usual—anywhere to be found. "S-s-s-see you in thirty."

"Yep," I said and I headed off.

Since knowing how to break submission holds is so crucial in the cage, after I'd skipped rope, done some sui-cide squats, and box jumped till it felt like my quads were burning streams of hot lava, I went to the mat for some specialized instruction in ground fighting.

"Two words," Nate-Neck said as the sweat poured from my body. "L-l-l-leg locks."

Nate-Neck gobbled me up in a one-legged X guard to show me the finer points of how to reverse out of it into a position of dominance by using my forearm for leverage. Fact is, once a fighter owns this kind of submission hold on a foe, he can take an opponent's ankle home with him to serve for dinner with soup, salad, and buttered bread if he wants.

Joint locks'll take down a Navy SEAL.

After a solid high-energy session on the mat with Nate-Neck, Klowner stepped in.

"How 'bout some love-tap time with a few Thai clinches?"

"Sure thing," I said.

Klowner began by showing me the proper way to snare an opponent. He always emphasized good technique because of how incredibly important it is in the cage. Sloppy street fighters, to a real pro, were easy to spot and even easier to beat.

"Forearms on the collarbone, arms around their neck, a tight, thumbless grip—wrist on wrist—around the back of the head, and keep your own elbows tight. You see how inside position rules and gives you the ability to turn your enemy's head like a steering wheel? You're in my Lexus right now."

Klowner snared my head like a black widow seizing its prey and whipped me side-to-side to give me a feel for how much control he actually held over me at the moment. He then began feeding me knee after knee to the body. It was as if my mid-section was a bass drum and he was being paid to bang away in a marching band.

"There's a little feather that'll tickle your pillow." Klowner drilled me in the ribs. "So, how's a fighter break this hold?"

"Forearm shiver to the face," I replied attempting to strike him in the temple.

"That's one way," Klowner said as he blocked my counterattack, his arms still wrapped like a python around my neck. He spun me left and delivered a thump to my body. "What else?"

"Drive my arm up through yours to gain control of the inside position and smash an uppercut to your nose," I answered, attempting to execute the move.

"Correct," Klowner replied. "But you know I ain't gonna let that happen." Klowner spun me right and kneed me in the midsection again to show me that he was still in firm control of the action. "What else ya got?"

"Use a lever move," I replied. "Step out, palm up under opponent's elbow, push up, and explode in the other direction."

"Great answer," Klowner said. "But when a fighter as big as me gets you in a Thai clinch, it ain't gonna be that easy."

Outweighing me by at least seventy pounds, towering over me six inches in height, Klowner wrapped his arms like a spider around my neck, and blow after blow blitzed my ribs as I struggled for a way out.

"Keep your head up while seeking a solution," he warned. "A knee smash to your nose will feel like I hit your brain with a fire hydrant."

"Got it."

"Any other ideas, M.D.?"

"I'm searching," I said, struggling from my position of disadvantage.

"Well, take your time," Klowner teased as he bombed me again with another knee. "I've got all day."

Even though I was the youngest in the gym and weighed the least, I never backed down from taking whatever hurt cards my training partners dealt out to me. Getting hit teaches a fighter to lose the fear of being hit; and the more times you're really smashed, the less fazed you are by the shock of it when the lights are on and you're center stage.

Plus, no one avoids getting clipped in this game. Not the heavyweights, not the veterans, not the ground game specialists or the fighters who view an impenetrable defense as a best choice for offense. Even the best take big shots. How a fighter handles these big shots is where victories are won.

"Say the word when you've had enough," Klowner offered.

I struggled without much luck to free myself from the hold. "You, too," I responded.

Klowner laughed. "All right, if you wanna be hardheaded about it." He whaled away some more. "Cootchey-cootchey-coo!"

As my midsection was being shelled by artillery, I grappled on, refusing to back down from the beating. Why? Because quitting becomes a habit. Give up once, you'll give up twice; and before you know it, you'll end up turning into a quitter who gives up entirely.

Me, I'll die before I'll quit. Surrender, to me, isn't an option.

"More scoops on your sundae?" Klowner asked. "Got some chocolate fudge sauce for ya, too."

Being that I was approaching the end of a long, grueling, strong-effort session, I was weakening. After all, there's only so much gas in any fighter's tank. However, that only made it more important for me to war on. Absorbing Klowner's knees had changed this workout from a physical one to a mental one. All good training sessions always exist at both levels anyway because the will to win is a muscle that needs exercise just like a bicep.

And if I ever needed any extra motivation to battle on, any added incentive to fight when it felt like all the fight had been drained from me, I simply visualized the one image that was never far from my thoughts.

Gemma. Her smiling face lit up my darkest days.

Klowner faked left, then drove his right knee into the center of my breastbone. There was a violent, thundering *BOOM!* It sounded as if someone had just dropped a two-hundred pound sandbag into the center of an empty room. The blow was so loud Nate-Neck set down his medicine ball and turned to see what had just happened.

There's a code among fighters who train in the same gym, an unspoken rule: they push one another, but nobody gets broken. Klowner relaxed the grip he'd held around my head, and I knew why. With his last shot, he knew he'd pushed it too close to the edge of what was acceptable.

I spun around and hammered him with a left hook to the liver. It caught Klowner flush.

"*Urgh,*" he groaned.

I backed away and raised my fists, ready to go some more. Every brawler knows you never drop your guard in the cage. It was a clean shot I'd nailed him with, and Klowner knew it.

He rubbed his side, then smiled. "I swear, this kid's got more heart than a Marine infantry," he said to Nate-Neck. "And I think his stomach muscles bruised my damn kneecap."

Nate-Neck grinned as Klowner turned and extended a glove. "Good work today, M.D."

We slapped hands. "Thanks."

"Yo, schoolboy, yo' punk-ass ready for a taste of me?"

Klowner and Nate-Neck spun around to see where the voice had come from, then dropped their eyes at the sight of the approaching fighter who was barking at me.

"Bam Bam wanna boogie?"

"G-g-g-give it a break, h-h-h-huh, Seize."

"Wut?" Seizure responded with a wicked smirk. "I just wanna work with the schoolboy on a few li'l choke holds."

Silverio "Seizure" DeSilva was a Brazilian jiu-jitsu expert in the Gracie line of fighters with the quickest hands in the gym. And the nastiest attitude. As an underground cage warrior who'd fought in Florida, Philly, and St. Louis, he had a sketchy, dark history of inducing seizures in his opponents through his signature rear naked choke hold. By cutting off the blood supply to other fighter's brains until they did a little epileptic dance in the center of the cage—which he'd then post on YouTube—he'd earned his nickname. These days, however, Seizure was a ranked professional who had given up the unsanctioned war circuit a few years ago and settled in Detroit, where he'd risen to number three in the middleweight division. Like so many others trying to scratch their way into the top tiers of MMA fighting, he'd stop at nothing to one day be a world champ.

Yet Seizure didn't take me seriously. He still viewed me from a big brother/little brother perspective.

At least he used to, until I knocked him into next Tuesday. That was a few months ago. Ever since then he's been extra chippy with me because word had leaked out around town that Bam Bam was actually gonna be the true prince of D-town cage fighting one day, and not Seizure.

"You still got some charge in those batteries, don't ya, schoolboy?" he taunted, wanting to spar.

The truth is, for years Seizure had always gotten extra rough with me whenever we went at it. Being that my natural body weight would one day take me into about the hundred and eighty-five–pound range when I was fully grown, he long ago realized we were on an eventual collision course for the middleweight title. That's probably why he always dished me out a few extra servings of "cage love" whenever we trained together, trying to get in my head early and plant seeds of doubt in my mind for later on down the road.

Loco would call him out on it too, telling Seizure to "stow that low-rent shit," but Seizure would just laugh it off, telling anyone who complained on my behalf that he was just doing me a favor by toughening me up for the big time.

However, a few months ago while Seizure was "toughening me up" with dirty-boxing elbows to the head, I caught him flush with a straight right hand that crossed his eyes and gave him an unobstructed view of the ceiling tiles.

"Seizure done been stunned!" Klowner hooted after I'd landed the big blow. "And it looks like the student is now the teacha!"

Even Loco, all five-foot-two, hundred and thirty-five pounds of him, smiled at the sight of his least favorite fighter in the gym lying flat on his back in the middle of the room, having been put there by the kid who mops the shower floor.

It wasn't a sexy punch that tanked him. In fact, the straight right hand is probably the most primitive, instinctual punch in human history. But I'd spied a weakness in the way Seizure used his aggressiveness, and everybody has a "button," a spot on their chin that if you hit it just right, night-night...they go down.

I'd simply found Seizure's button. However, for him to have a kid like me knock him from Detroit to Pluto in front of everyone was a big blow to his ego. Whipping my ass publicly had since become an itch for him that he desperately wanted to scratch.

"I still got plenty of juice," I said, even though I'd just finished up my third hour of training with two human tanks.

"Then let's go," Seizure said smashing his gloves together. "I got a little sumptin' sumptin' I wanna show ya."

Seizure began to shake his body as if he were mocking an epileptic, then he ripped his hand across his throat making a sinister "slicing the jugular" gesture.

"Ready, punk?" Seizure jumped into my face and stared with menace, hungry to spill my blood.

He moved close. Too close. So close that I could smell the nasty garlic noodles he'd had for lunch on his warm, horrid breath.

"Can't," I said maintaining eye contact with him for an extra second before glancing away. The clock on the wall read three forty. "Maybe another time."

I took off my gloves, stepped off of the mat and grabbed the laundry hamper filled with towels, figuring I'd empty them for Loco before I left to go pick up my sister. Didn't matter what kind of trash talk Seizure threw at me, there was no way I was letting a kindergarten-age little girl walk home alone from school down East Seven Mile by herself.

"Aw, where ya goin', Bam Bam?" Seizure teased. "Afraid to dance with a sexy li'l partner like me?"

I didn't respond.

"'Cause you know what I'm gonna do to ya once we go back at it, right? Right? RIGHT?"

Not answering seemed to get under Seizure's skin, so I remained quiet. Why not play a few head games with him, really piss him off, I thought. Silently, I lifted the dirty towel basket.

"Yo, one sec, schoolboy," Seizure commanded. Then he grabbed a towel, placed a finger over his right nostril and blew out a stringy, slimy booger from his left.

A moment later he switched sides and horked out a nasty yellowish line of snot from his right.

Then he gargled up a loogie, spit into the towel, wiped all the foulness from his face, and called out, "Bank shot."

Seizure tossed the rag. It bounced against my chest then dropped into the laundry basket.

"Two points, schoolboy," he said with a smile.

I glared.

"Wut? I'm right here, bitch. You want some of dis?"

I glanced at the clock again. Three forty-two p.m.

Dealing with Seizure would have to wait. Towel basket in hand, I turned and left.

"You're d-d-d-disgusting, Seize."

"That's right, Neck. I'm one hell of a nasty man!" Seizure threw a mock right-left combo then made another slashing sign across his throat. "We gonna have our dance date, Bam Bam," he yelled at me. "That's a fuckin' promise."

FOUR

When I showed up at school the next day a bunch of people were wishing me "Congrats." Wasn't sure why though. My next fight wasn't till Saturday. When I got to fourth period, however, Mr. Freedman filled in the blanks.

"Looks like you are better at bingo than you thought, son."

"Excuse me?"

"Guess who won a spot in the charter school lottery."

"Give it to someone else."

Disbelief flashed across Mr. Freedman's eyes. "Pardon me?"

I took my seat. He'd heard me. Far as I was concerned, our conversation was over.

Two girls sitting behind me sharing a bag of chips laughed at an inside joke about a bucktooth girl sitting in the front row. A skinny boy on my left wearing a blue-and-orange striped shirt put his head down and prepared to take his regular, late-morning nap. I took out a pencil and my notebook and got ready for the start of class. It'd be stupid for me to accept something like that, I thought. Let it go to someone who could do something with the opportunity, someone who could make something positive come out it.

My path was set. Had been for years and there was no changing it. I wasn't complaining. It was just a cold, hard fact.

Mr. Freedman's eyes locked in on me from the front of the room. I avoided his gaze and stared at the marked-up wall to my left. Someone ought to paint this dump, I thought. How's a person supposed to concentrate on science when it says **LICKY MY BALL-BALLS** two feet away?

Of course, my dad would never let me go anyway. Hell, he wants me to drop out right now. What does a kid like you need with school? he says. Being that I'm gonna make a living with my fists, the sooner I start to train full-time like a real professional, the better.

In fact, the only reason I'm still going to school is because the truant officers for tenth grade are such pains-in-the-asses that my dad doesn't want them "gettin' all involved with his bizness." What he means by that is he doesn't want them calling social services on him like they've already done a bunch of times before. One more bad visit from a city social worker, and I could find myself in some foster care situation.

Separated from Gemma.

No way I'm gonna let that happen. However, come eleventh grade, next year, he wants me the hell outta here.

"A high school dropout in D-town? There be a million

of those," he says, his plan already figured out. "Ain't no truant office gonna blink an eye next year 'cause it ain't really even about the parents then. It's about you, and if they come here askin' questions, I'll be like, 'But I wanted him to stay in school, too, Officer. Me and you, we're like, on the same fuckin' side.'"

My father chuckled. He had the kind of chuckle that only sinners at the devil's dinner table possessed.

I'd actually stumbled across this idea about my dad's sinister laugh one day when my mind was drifting in church and I found myself about to nod off while staring at a colorful painting on the wall. See, my mother used to take us to Holy Grace Church every Sunday morning at nine. In the picture, I noticed that all the good people were hurting and sad and crying in pain and all the bad folks were laughing and having the time of their lives.

Just like my dad, I'd thought.

I'd stopped going to church after my mom left, though. Been thinking about going back but then again, been thinking about not goin' back, too. Really, why bother? Did I really need a weekly reminder that people who tried to be good always got screwed over?

When it came to school, however, my dad was spot-on. With budget resources so limited in Detroit, tenth grade really was the last year the system could afford to even try to keep a kid like me in class. Come eleventh grade, they stopped pretending to try to prevent kids such as myself from falling through the cracks.

Naw, no way was I attending some fancy charter school

where sissy-boys got manicures and ate fruit-flavored yogurt during nutrition breaks. My road belonged to the hard asphalt of the caged warrior.

I could see by the way he was staring at me that Mr. Freedman wasn't happy about my decision. Not happy one bit.

I just hoped he could see that I didn't really give a damn. What the hell did he know about all the problems I was sweatin' anyway?

The bell rang to begin class, and even though I was looking at the front board for the entire period, I didn't hear one thing Mr. Freedman said. All I could think about was getting to Loco'z as soon as fourth period ended so I could go mash.

Some days, a dude just wants to explode.

■   ■   ■

"Leverage, M.D.!" my dad screamed between rounds of my next fight. "Find his vulnerability and exploit it."

"Dad," I said sucking hard to regain my breath after the third round. "This dude's got a beard."

"Life gives you cards, you play 'em. No excuses, son. Leverage, leverage, leverage."

Easy for him to say, I thought. I mean, why the hell would he even set up a fight like this for me, with some out-of-town, shaved-head muscle-monster from New Orleans, who musta had fifty pounds, five inches, and a giant reach advantage over me?

Of course, I knew why. The answer was obvious.

Money.

In Detroit, local talent for me to face was starting to dry up. My rep had grown too big and I'd beaten too many of D-town's best maulers, so the Priests had started to import guys for me to fight.

"Find his vulnerability, apply leverage, and exercise your will on this orangutan-lookin' mothafucker."

I sucked in another deep breath and prepared to head out for Round Four.

"Yes, sir," I answered.

In Round One between me and Beard Man, I'd decided to take him to the ground right out of the gate to try to neutralize his reach advantage, and almost all of our opening action was spent grappling, with me looking for a submission hold to try to force a tap out. I almost snared his left wrist at one point in a kamakubi, a gooseneck-style wristlock that bouncers use when escorting drunks out of late-night bar fights.

Even King Kong would tap out if he got snared in a kamakubi. Fuzzy Face, however, had some decent wrestling skills, and I wasn't able to seal the deal on the hold.

I'd tried the same ground-attack strategy in Round Two, but again nothing stuck; so for Round Three I decided to stay on my feet and play the counterstrike game to see what might come of that.

It had cost me. I'd taken two back-to-back heavy shots to my left eye during the round, and while I could deal with the pain, the swelling had started to cloud my vision.

Worse, though, was that my cornerman didn't have an enswell with him, that small piece of frozen metal used by cut men to reduce inflammation in facial injuries. If my father had had one, simply applying light pressure with it would have reduced the swelling and let me fight on without a handicap. However, my dad had "forgotten" to refill his supply bag after our last bout—truth is, earlier I didn't even see him bring a trainer's kit into the arena with him—and my eyeball was beginning to puff like a bloated purple water balloon.

Without ice, it wouldn't be long before my left eye was the size of a California orange. And entirely shut. Dancing with Grizzly Adams was hard enough with full vision, but if this match got into Round Five or beyond, I'd be fighting half blind.

I had no choice but to take a risk. My eyesight was already blurred, and the involuntary twitches from my left eye easily telegraphed to my opponent where he should target his attack.

The buzz of the crowd grew more and more electric. Could it be, they had to wonder, if this was the night that the undefeated Bam Bam finally went down?

"Vulnerability!" my father shouted from behind the fence. "Find this testicle gargler's vulnerability and leverage it to your advantage!"

My dad wasn't a man anybody ever accused of being intelligent in everyday life, but when it came to fighting, I had to admit, he knew his stuff. Between rounds, he talked to me about how openings always appeared for the patient fighter; but figuring out this guy's weak spot would only come for me inside the heat and flow of battle. In fights like this, he'd said, fluidity, smarts, and improv were the keys to victory. My scripted plans would be out the window.

With the twitching, cloudiness, and swelling growing worse and worse, I needed to do something quick. The clock was ticking on my eye.

Yes, that was it. Suddenly, the answer came to me. I'd dangle my eye out there like a steak and lure the assface in to tempt him to go for a kill shot. His vulnerability would be an irresistible urge to attack my vulnerability.

After all, I've seen Shark Week a thousand times on TV. When you hang bloody tuna over the side of a boat, you know it's only a matter of time before the great whites come calling. Same thinking applied here. Instead of protecting my injured face, which would be the natural thing to do, I'd offer it up to the son of a bitch like a Halloween treat to set a trap.

If my plan worked, I'd go for a shin choke and twist his neck like a piece of licorice. And if that didn't work and I got jammed up, I was probably looking at a detached retina, maybe even a broken eye socket.

Sometimes cage fighting boils down to risk versus reward. With my eye growing puffier and more swollen by the second, the time had come to take a chance. It was clear I'd have to gamble.

Only problem was, I hated gambling.

We began the fourth on our feet exchanging leg strikes, but to set my trap, I knew I'd need to get us to the ground with Whisker Man on top of me, thinking he held a superior position.

Luring him into having an apparently dominant position wasn't too hard, because most fighters will grab the top if they can. In a half butterfly guard, I lay on my back, playing defense.

And I avoided taking any big shots on the way down, too. Thank goodness. One big strike to my already damaged face and I'd be done. My eye would pop like a zit.

He threw an elbow. I blocked it.

He threw a hook. I warded it off and countered with a short, straight right.

On my back in a classic defensive position, I wrapped my knees around his midsection and held him close so he couldn't get the space he needed to pummel me with a furious storm of fists and elbows. Then I turned my head slightly to the right and showed him my battered left eye. He lasered in on it like a tiger salivating for gazelle flesh, but being so tightly locked in my guard prevented him from being able to fire off any meaningful shots.

I could feel his frustration grow as he searched for a way to create some striking distance. The more space between our chests, the more room he'd have to launch a hurricane.

That's when I went for the kimura, one of the most common submission holds fighters usually go for when you're on the bottom.

Or so I made him think.

I tried to reach for his right arm, and he dipped his shoulder to prevent the kimura. Quick as a rattlesnake, I passed my leg over his shoulder, pressed my shin against his windpipe, and trapped the back of his head in a vise lock, making a figure-four with my legs around his neck.

The crowd exploded! It was the first gogoplata I'd ever landed, a sickening choke hold that, once owned, only ever offers one final chapter to any fight's story.

Tap out. Mister Face Fuzz slapped the side of my leg in surrender before I permanently crushed his windpipe. I released. My eye the size of a grapefruit, my head throbbing with pain, questions as to whether I'd ever even see clearly again from the left side of my face, victory was mine.

My dad rushed into the cage. "Only a fool would bet against my son," my father shouted, his arms raised as the crowd cheered. "Only a mothafuckin' fool!"

As the crowd still buzzed with excitement about the raw, violent drama they'd just witnessed, Weasel approached. "Top-notch fight, kid. Top-notch fight." Weasel dipped his head and then inspected my eye. "Whoa. You wanna ice bag or something, Bam Bam?"

"What he wants is his cash," my father said, answering for me. Weasel, an unlit cigarette propped behind his ear, reached into his black leather jacket and withdrew a white envelope that my dad immediately snatched.

"It's all there, Demon, it's all there." Despite Weasel's assurances, my father began counting the money. Five grand for an out-of-state conquest plus another six grand for my dad's bets on the side. "Priests always pay. You know that, Demon. Priests always pay." Weasel paused.

"But the Priests always get paid, too. Remember that, Demon—the Priests always get paid, too."

My father stopped flipping through the stack of hundred dollar bills and glared. He knew Weasel was talking about the fact that my father had been flying naked on his wagers.

Flying naked yet again.

"Whatcha trying to say, Weasel?"

"Top-notch, fight, kid," Weasel responded, knowing he'd already made his point. "Top-notch fight."

One of the cage-side girls whose job it was to get beers, provide smokes, and flirt with big spenders by jiggling her jugs caught my father's eye.

"Hey," he shouted. "Whose ass does my son have to kiss to get a hot-damn bag of ice 'round here?"

The cage girl stared at my father with a look of, *Uhm, you talkin' to me?*

"Let's go," my dad snapped, clapping his hands together. "Chop, chop, bitch. You lookin' at a future title belt holder. Multiple weight classes, too." My father handed me three hundred dollars. "Love your heart, M.D. That shit is what real champions is made of."

FIVE

I had no idea how many Priests there were in the entire organization, but I did know that there was only one High Priest in all the land. He was a black man with a permanent scowl who always wore sunglasses, even indoors at night.

I waited off to the side, a towel draped over my shoulders, while my father had a private conversation with His Holiness. Once they were finished talking, my dad approached and informed me of some news.

"Tonight, we eat steak."

I laughed at his enthusiasm. "Steak?" I said. "Come on, you know I don't really eat much red meat."

"Bullshit," my dad replied. "A fighter needs his iron. A good hunka flesh in your belly is just what the doctor ordered for that eye." My dad slapped me proudly on the back and then squeezed my shoulders with an affectionate pinch. "My treat, bay-bee."

The victory over the out-of-town brawler with the big rep followed by the conversation with the High Priest had put my father in one of his good moods. He knew that my walking through one door would lead to others being opened. Already the Priests were talking about raising the stakes for my next fight.

And raising the stakes, of course, meant raising the payouts. Raising the payouts would raise my profile. And all that raising raised my father's spirits. According to my dad, it was time to celebrate.

"We done earned it," he said. "Go get yo' ass cleaned up."

I showered and changed, but instead of heading home to relieve Mrs. McCullough, Gem's babysitter, my dad and I jumped into his dinged-up four-door Lincoln, its black paint scratched, the passenger side mirror held on with strands of silver duct tape, and we drove into downtown to enjoy a late-night meal fit for a soon-to-be cage king.

"You know, one day," my father said to me as he sipped a freshly refilled glass of Chivas Regal, "we gonna own us a li'l beach house on the Cayman Islands."

"The Cayman Islands?"

"Yep," he said. "The Cayman Fuckin' Islands." Dad leaned back in the steakhouse chair like he owned the whole damn restaurant. "I tell ya, the beaches there got white sand and water so warm the ocean feels like a bathtub. Not polluted or no shit, neither. We're talking double-clear blue with fish swimming by your toes, like the kind you only catch sight of in one of them rich people's tropical tanks."

"You been there before?" I asked. A sandy blond waitress wearing a tight black dress served me spinach salad. Dad, in additional to a second scotch, was presented with a chilled lump meat crab cocktail.

And cracked lobster claws. Since he couldn't make up his mind which appetizer he wanted when we first ordered, he'd simply ordered both.

"Been there once," he told me. "Went there to be a sparring partner for Meldrick Taylor when he was welterweight champ. Brought in by Don King."

"You knew Don King?" I asked. "THE Don King? The guy with the crazy hair who used to manage Mike Tyson?"

"Now, I didn't say I knew him," my dad answered as he dunked a hunk of white-and-red lobster meat in a dish of melted butter. "But his peoples brought me in to work out their boy."

"Did you?" I asked. "I mean, like, did ya take it to him?"

"Never got the chance," my dad answered. "Flew me all that way and their fighter never even made it to the compound. Some shit about training camp changing locations or whatever. But I did get to see a glimpse."

"A glimpse?" I asked. "Of what?"

"A glimpse of the life," my dad responded, a dreamy look in his eyes. "I saw the way a world champion gets to live. Traveling by private jet. Changing cars like other men change shoes. Houses, clothes, giant suites in luxury hotels with butlers and servants and shit. That's what I want for you, son. The best." He reached out and tapped my cheek affectionately. "'Cause the best deserves the best."

My father then spun around in his chair to address the nearby busboy. "Oh hey, boss man, send our waitress on over here a sec, would ya."

The restaurant's busboy, dressed in a white shirt with a black tie and black pants, stopped midway through setting down a fork on a table behind us and replied, "Right away, sir," then dashed off.

"That's what I like about fancy restaurants—they know how to properly talk to a mothafucker." My dad took another sip of Chivas then turned his attention to the crab.

"*Oooh-weee*, and the women," he said continuing his train of thought. A large, delicious grin crossed his face. "You can't believe the way a world champion gets poontang. You gettin' yourself a good taste of tail, M.D.?"

"Dad," I said a little bashful.

"What, I'm serious," he responded. "A fella like you should have all kinds of bitches throwing themselves your way."

I think he could tell by the look in my eye that I wasn't too big a fan of guys always referring to girls as "bitches."

"Oh, excuse me," he said apologetically catching wind of my disapproval. "I mean hos." He smiled and then stabbed a bite of the lump meat crab with his long silver fork. "Nah, just kiddin'. But you know what I'm talking about, M.D. Don't avoid the question. You gettin' laid or what?"

Yep, I did know what he was talking about. Knew it too well. Girls threw themselves at me all the time. Had been doing it for years now, too. Hell, I'd lost my virginity at age twelve to a sixteen-year-old, all because I was Bam Bam the cage warrior.

"Girls are crazy these days. I mean, just so aggressive," I

said to my dad. Using my fork I flipped an unwanted crouton out of my salad. "Truth is," I reluctantly admitted, "it kinda turns me off."

"What?" my dad said, semi-shocked. "Oh, lemme guess, you want a re-lay-shun-ship?" I could tell the pricey booze was starting to get to him by the way he teased me.

"Look," he said, getting more serious. "You and I never done had no talk about the birds and bees and shit, so I'm gonna give ya some advice. Not about fucking, of course," he said. "'Cause Mother Nature will take care of that. A blind ass monkey can fuck. But about women."

Our waitress approached the table. "Yes, sir?"

"Another one of these, please," my dad said holding up his near-empty glass. "And one for my boy, too."

She paused.

"That a problem?" my dad asked.

"Uhm," the waitress said. "I think I'm gonna need to see some ID, please."

"He don't need no fucking ID. Just get his ass a drink."

"Sir, I, uhm..." The waitress fumbled for a polite response. "Without ID, we're not allowed to serve..."

"Look, bitch..."

"Forget it, Dad," I interjected before his temper could kick in. "You know me. I won't drink it anyway." I waved my hand up and down my body. "Keepin' the temple pure, that sorta thing."

"You sure?" my father asked. I could tell he was ready to slap the waitress across the room if that's what needed to be done in order to get me my glass of scotch. After all, it's not like he hadn't hit women before.

"Yeah, I'm sure," I said.

"All right, suit yourself," he replied. "But I still want mine." My father raised his eyes and glared at our server. "Unless you think you need to see some ID from me, too."

"Right away, sir." The waitress in the tight black dress scampered away. My dad watched as her ass wiggled across the dining room floor.

"Man, I'd like to eat a bite of that. *Mm!* Now, where was I?" He finished the last of his crab, gulped the last of his lobster, reached for a piece of bread, covered it with butter and then chomped. "Oh, yeah," he said. "Relationships. They're for suckers. Only get a fighter in trouble and make him lose his focus."

"Well, no worries, 'cause I ain't in one."

"Good," he said. "That's real good. 'Cause remember this, son, and remember it good." He downed the last of his drink. "Relationships'll just fuck a man up."

"I've got another Chivas Regal, neat, splash of lime," the waitress said, setting down my father's drink. "A filet mignon, medium-well in peppercorn sauce, side of baked potato, loaded, extra bacon bits, extra sour cream." She set down my father's plate. "And a grilled New York strip rare, side of steamed broccoli, no sauce, no salt for the young gentleman."

"Thank you," I replied as she set down my food. "And some more water, please."

"Of course." She looked toward the busboy and he dashed off. Within moments, my glass was full. "Will there be anything else?" our waitress asked.

"Yeah," my father said. "Your cell phone number, sweetie, 'cause after this steak you lookin' *mmm-mmm* good for dessert."

My father cackled. He was serious.

"Enjoy your meal," the waitress replied coolly, trying to remain professional.

Not caring one bit that she knew he was watching her ass, my father's eyes followed the wiggle of her butt all the way across to the other side of the dining room. Once she was out of view, he picked up a large, silver, extremely sharp knife and cut his perfectly grilled meat.

"But you bein' the relationship type," he said as he carved himself a hunk of the restaurant's most expensive dish. "I gotta say, M.D. that shit makes me worried." He jammed a two-inch piece of wet with blood, reddish-pink, charcoal striped steak into his face and chewed with his mouth open. "Makes me wonder if you got the killa instinct."

"You ain't gotta worry about that," I replied.

"I don't?"

"You don't."

We looked into each other's eyes, and there was a pause.

"Yeah, well," he said. "We'll see about that."

Indeed we will, I thought. Indeed we will.

SIX

At school on Monday my eye felt better. Spending Sunday on the couch watching football with a few squirts of contusion cream and two bags of frozen peas pressed against my face had reduced the swelling, and since I hadn't been cut, there were no lacerations or gashes to worry about. Aside from a nasty bruise that was still tender, my vision wasn't blurry, and the headaches, though pounding, weren't the worst I'd ever had to deal with. Overall, aside from the fact that it probably wasn't too good an idea to do any upside-down handstand push-ups this week—because inversions could cause internal eye pressure that might give me problems down the road—I'd escaped from Saturday night's war in fairly decent shape.

Not all cage fighters can always say the same. Once I saw a kid get carried out of the coop with a pool of blood flowing from their head and one eyeball dangling from an empty, hollow socket attached by only a few thin shreds of meaty string. Though being in the MMA game teaches a warrior not to let the injuries of other brawlers get to you emotionally, when I saw how this fighter's face had been pummeled into dog food, I couldn't help but feel bad for her.

Guy fights get brutal; girl fights get savage.

"Yeah, uhm, like they need one of yo' students down in the 'ministrative center," said an office aide who had just entered my second period class without bothering to knock. The girl, tight jeans, tight sweater, about sixteen, wearing a fluffy pink scarf, took a moment to suck her cherry lollipop. "You gots a..." She paused. "Oh, damn," she said, almost as if speaking to herself. "They want Bam Bam."

Apparently, the girl hadn't bothered to read the name on the blue note card the office had handed to her until now. And now that she'd realized who it was she'd been asked to go get out of class, her whole face lit up.

"Who do they want, young lady?" asked Mrs. Dooley, my hunched-over, white-haired history teacher. Mrs. Dooley was so old, I think she'd actually witnessed the Civil War.

"They want McCutcheon," the girl replied, smiling big and bright. "McCutcheon Daniels."

Without getting up from behind her desk, Mrs. Dooley pointed in my direction and then pointed at the door. "And take your stuff," she ordered.

I grabbed my things and headed out.

"What do they want?" I asked the office aide.

"Probably just some stupid shit," the girl said as we exited the room and walked the halls. "I means I ain't even realize till just now that it was like you they wanted."

"But you don't know what it's about?" I said.

"Nope," she replied taking another suck off of her lollipop, slow and suggestive. "Hey, lemme ask you a question," she said as we walked side-by-side toward the office. She was practically batting her eyelashes at me.

"Yeah?"

"Do you believe in horoscopes?"

"Horoscopes?" I asked. "Like astrology?"

"Uh-huh," she said. "'Cause, like, I was reading my horoscope last weekend and it said that love was gonna soon be walking right through my door and then like, this happened and wow."

"What happened?"

"Me and you," she answered as if it wasn't the most obvious thing in the world.

"But I didn't walk through your door," I said. "You kinda walked through mine."

"Yeah, well, ain't the stars funny?" She smiled in a cutesy, flirty way. "You wanna go somewhere?"

"Go somewhere?" I asked. "What, like now?"

"Sure. Why not?"

"Uhm, thanks," I said, taking the blue hall pass from her hand. "But I better go see what this is about. Maybe another time."

"Not anotha time, Bam Bam," she told me, putting her hand on her hip and leaning to her left in an unmistakably sexual way. "For you, anytime."

I cracked a smile, pretending I was flattered because I didn't want to hurt her feelings, but the truth is I was glad she'd stopped walking with me and our conversation had ended. The bigger my rep grew, the more people were less interested in me, McCutcheon, and the more they were grabbing for any ol' pieces of Bam Bam the warrior that they could get their hands on.

Now I knew how that waitress from the other night felt, I thought as I made my way through the school halls. Just a hunk of meat.

"Is that him?" asked an elegant-looking white lady wearing a powder-blue dress as soon I crossed through the large double doors at the front of our main office. Principal Porter, a plump African American man with a thin mustache and shiny silver belt buckle, wasn't sure. He looked to his left for an answer.

Mr. Freedman nodded. "It is."

"McCutcheon," Principal Porter said, rising to his feet to greet me. "Step inside my office, won't you?"

"Yes, sir."

I was led down a skinny hall that looked like the last time it had been decorated was thirty years ago. A variety of rah-rah school posters, yellowed, with pictures of kids in clothing styles and haircuts long since outdated, hung on the wall. Before entering through the last door on the right, I spied a picture of a former cheerleader who had been murdered in a drive-by shooting seven years ago.

Her front tooth had been blackened out by a dark marker and someone had scrawled SUCK ME on her forehead.

Students at Fenkell just got no respect for nothing.

"Please, sit," Principal Porter said as he pointed to one of the worn blue chairs to the right of his large desk, covered with Post-it notes. This was the first time I'd ever spoken to our school principal, the first time I'd even seen the inside of his office. Sure, every student in the school knew the principal's name—but how and why did he all of a sudden know mine?

Didn't take Sherlock Holmes, though, to figure out that this musta had something to do with bingo.

Each of the three adults took a seat surrounding me. Or at least it felt like they were surrounding me, even though I could sense that all of them were going to try to be nice. One by one, each took a good look at my banged-up left eye. My guess was they'd decided not to say anything about it in order to get the meeting off to a good start.

I could tell they wanted to mention it, though. Thing is, with face injuries, after a few days they often end up looking much worse than they actually are.

"McCutcheon, can you please explain something to me?" Principal Porter began. "You won a spot in the charter school lottery and yet you've informed Mr. Freedman that you are not going to accept it. I mean, you do realize the highly unique opportunity being presented to you, don't you?"

I didn't answer. Mostly because it felt like it was one of those questions that wasn't really a question at all, but more like a statement. And when any answer you give won't be good enough, I think it's best to just to keep your mouth shut.

The well-dressed white lady, her spine straight, her blue eyes clear and focused, continued to study me.

"Not a child in this city's ever turned down an offer like this before," Principal Porter continued. "Between the scholarship you'll be given, the resources and the support you'll be provided, you're saying no? Pardon me for saying so, but it makes no sense."

The three of them waited for a reply. What could I say? Not really having an answer that would satisfy them, I played with the drawstring of my hoodie.

"You know, I've done a bit of digging," Mr. Freedman said as he took out a piece of paper with the school logo at the top and began to read from it. "An inspection of all your grades, McCutcheon, reveals an interesting pattern."

He handed me a printout of my records.

Grade Report: Daniels, McCutcheon ID#: A0486632

Period 1	A
Period 2	A-
Period 3	A
Period 4	A
Lunch (B session)	
Period 5	F
Period 6	F
Period 7	F

"Periods one through four are all As and periods five, six, and seven are all Fs," he noted.

Principal Porter took the sheet of information and examined it. "Why?" he asked me.

I fiddled some more with the drawstrings on my hoodie

but remained silent. Mr. Freedman, seeing that my words would be few if any, took a shot at explaining it all for me.

"Because McCutcheon never shows up to any of those classes," he said. "After lunch every day, he's ditching."

Principal Porter didn't look shocked to hear news that one of his students was skipping class. In a school with so few security guards, so many corners to hide in, and such beaten-down facilities, there were always lots of kids out roaming campus when they were supposed to be in class. Ditchers were like roaches at Fenkell; every time you turned on a new light or opened a new door, fresh ones appeared.

Besides, the list of kids with three Fs or more on their report card was probably longer than the list of kids without three or more Fs on their report card at our school. By at least a two-to-one ratio. D-town wasn't called ground zero for America's public schools for nothing.

"Care to explain what is going on, son?" Mr. Freedman asked.

My silence somehow inspired the white lady in the powder-blue dress to make a decision.

"Mr. Daniels will be coming with me," she said in a firm that-will-be-that tone. She then picked up her purse and stood. It was clear that wherever she was going, she planned to take me with her.

"What? Where?" I asked.

"To visit Radiance."

"Now?"

Her penetrating blue eyes locked in on me. "Clearly, you are intelligent, McCutcheon," she said to me. "Now, let's just hope that you are intelligent enough to recognize exactly what you'd be missing."

"But right now?" I asked again.

Slowly, she looked at her thin, silver wristwatch and read the black Roman numerals on its face. "It's eleven seventeen a.m., Mr. Daniels. Do you have somewhere else you're supposed to be?"

It was like she was daring me to spill my secret. I mean, of course I had somewhere else. Loco'z by twelve thirty.

Every day meant training by twelve thirty.

I turned to Mr. Freedman. Then to the principal. Then back to the lady who'd come out of nowhere.

I was boxed in and she knew it.

"I'll have you back before the school day is over, Mr. Daniels. You can resume your 'activities' then."

Leverage, I thought. She had it.

I rose from my chair. Sometimes, you just have to tap out. It was off to Radiance.

"By the way," she said to me as she opened the door of a gleaming, brand-new BMW. I climbed inside the passenger seat and the sweet smell of luxurious leather hit me. I'd never been inside a BMW before. Every inch of her car glistened. "My name is Mrs. Notley," she informed me. "I'm the headmistress of Radiance Academy."

"So, like, you're in charge?"

"No," she replied. "God is in charge." Mrs. Notley pushed the ignition and the car roared to life. "But I am most indubitably second-in-command."

SEVEN

A manicured lawn. Spires on the buildings. A campus without any steel fences surrounding it like a prison yard. Though it was only a twenty-five-minute ride to Radiance, it felt like we'd arrived in a different universe.

Mrs. Notley and I walked up the front steps, white as snow, that led into the main building, also painted gleaming white. I spied a plaque on the wall by the door, small but impressive looking. Curious, I went over to read it.

PUGNARE AD CONSEQUI, CONSEQUI AD DA
FIGHT TO ACHIEVE, ACHIEVE TO GIVE

"It's more than a motto," Mrs. Notley commented. "It's a way of life."

I tried to remember if our school had a motto. I think it was *Go Panthers,* or something like that.

We went inside, and Mrs. Notley began to spell out all the benefits her school could offer. The extensive and diverse curriculum; the wealth of resources like an Olympic pool, full orchestra, and theater; and the one-hundred-percent success rate of the Radiance senior class being accepted to four-year colleges. Suddenly we stopped and she poked her head inside a classroom.

"Come, take a look," Mrs. Notley said, motioning me in. Perhaps it was a coincidence, perhaps not, but the class she'd selected for me to see was science, my favorite subject.

We entered a room without any desks, just lab tables and workstations with black office chairs that had wheels on them so that the students could slide around and easily move from one location to another. None of the kids seemed even to notice that their principal had just come into the room. Weird, I thought. Most kids usually snap to attention when big shots enter a classroom, but these students seemed not to have noticed.

And they weren't pretending, either; they were just too caught up in their work.

I scanned the class. Most of the students were huddled in small groups, some around microscopes, others around tablet computers, all working or talking or reading or writing. And not one kid had his or her head down taking a mid-morning nap.

I looked at the front board.

Who murdered Mrs. Stephanie DeAngelo?
- **How?**
- **Where?**
- **When?**
- **Why?**
EVIDENCE! EVIDENCE! EVIDENCE!

"Oh, good morning, Mrs. Notley." I turned and saw a short woman carrying a big beige box. She looked so pregnant it seemed as though she might pop by lunch. "Excuse me," she said. I stepped aside and reached to hold open the door for her so she could more easily enter the room.

"Thank you," she said waddling by.

Was that the teacher, I wondered? Not even inside with the class? At Fenkell, if a teacher left a room filled with students without any supervision you could be damn sure that by time she got back somebody would have been either tied up, bleeding, or set on fire.

"Good morning, Mrs. Clascus," Mrs. Notley replied. "Is this the new forensics unit?"

"Yes, crime scene analysis. Those students over there are analyzing DNA blood samples; in the back corner they're working with fingerprinting; to the left we're co-teaching with math by having them look at the verification of evidence using Newton's Law of Cooling and . . ." The teacher stopped mid-sentence and then called out to the entire class. "Okay people, I've got your hair samples." She set down the beige box. "Each team needs to send up a representative. And not in five minutes but NOW."

A moment later plastic bags of human hair were being distributed to each of the group representatives who'd rushed over. Being preggers didn't seem to slow this woman down one bit.

"Uhm, Jennie," Mrs. Clascus asked seeing that she still had one bag of hair that hadn't been handed out. "Aren't you sending up a teammate?" Mrs. Clascus waved the bag at this Jennie in a "come and get it" manner.

A girl in a black sleeveless top lifted her eye from a microscope. "No need, Mrs. C."

The teacher paused, unsure. A few students quieted down to listen in. Apparently everyone here was like some sort of student detective.

Jennie exchanged a knowing glance with three other kids—her teammates, I assumed. They all silently debated whether or not to share some secret with the rest of the room. A moment later Jennie shrugged and announced, "Not to spoil your weekend plans, everybody, but as it turns out, Mrs. Stephanie DeAngelo wore a wig."

"WHAT!?" A giant groan echoed through the room as if hours of valuable time working on some aspect of this project had just been lost.

And more importantly, hours' more worth of new work now seemed to be ahead for these teams. Hours of work that would snatch up their weekend.

Mrs. Clascus smiled. "I knew they'd figure it out at some point," she said to Mrs. Notley about her scheme to misdirect the class and try to get their scent off the real murderer's trail. "I just thought it would take them until next week."

The class buzzed with this new information, and each of the teams threw themselves deeply back into their work trying to calculate the consequences of this new knowledge on their case.

"This is McCutcheon," Mrs. Notley said to Mrs. Clascus, introducing me.

"Hey," she said. "New student here?"

"He's considering it," Mrs. Notley told her.

"Know anything about anatomy?" the pregnant teacher asked me. "Bones, blood, blunt objects forcefully striking the human head?"

"Um, a little," I answered.

"Well, you're here at a good time then. It's dead body week." Mrs. Clascus turned and called out to her class again. "All right people, means, motive, and opportunity. Without those, you have no case." I looked back out into the room. Jennie, the girl in the black sleeveless top, buried her eye in her microscope, then called two teammates over to take a look at something she'd just discovered. I wondered what they saw.

"Gotta go," Mrs. Clascus said. "More tricks up my sleeve." The teacher slyly smiled then waddled off. It was like she was having more fun than any kid in the room.

"Come, let's head to my office," Mrs. Notley said to me as she opened the door and escorted me out. Minutes later I was sitting in an oversized chocolate brown leather chair with creases that cracked each time I moved.

"Radiance Academy was founded in 1853." Mrs. Notley poured herself a cup of coffee. Wisps of steam rose as the black drink filled her white cup.

And no, I wasn't offered any.

"Originally we were a private institution, but after the

Great Depression, the board of directors converted it to a public school to better serve the community." My eyes wandered around her large office. This lady owned more books than anyone I'd ever seen.

"We became one of Michigan's first charter schools quite some time ago, but with the past decade's budget cuts, we've been forced to morph into an innovatively funded public/private hybrid model, with a waiting list that exceeds one thousand students per year."

I guess she expected me to be impressed.

I wasn't.

"You know," Mrs. Notley leaned forward, my laid-back attitude not doing much to impress her, "you might have won the lottery, Mr. Daniels, and that might not mean much to you, but now that you've had your number pulled, you should know one thing."

"What's that?"

"It means something to me. I want you here. And I'm one of those persnickety old ladies that almost always gets what she wants."

She took a small sip of her coffee. No sugar, no milk; she drank it black. I shifted in my chair and the leather seat creaked again. "Do you know what the word persnickety means, McCutcheon?" Her blue eyes lasered in on me. "It means I am a pushy pain in the gluteus maximus."

Mrs. Notley reached for a bell, a small one that sat on the flat surface of her polished desk, and rang it. A moment later, the door opened behind me.

"McCutcheon, I'd like you to meet one of our finest students, Kaitlyn Cummings."

I turned around and WOW! one of the hottest girls I'd ever seen entered the room.

Tall, athletic, a look of intelligence and confidence in her eyes. And that white schoolgirl uniform with the plaid skirt, well...it looked like Radiance had a few more campus resources than I'd originally realized.

I had to laugh to myself. *Aw, looks like Miss Persnickety's siccing the big dogs on me now.*

"Kaitlyn is our top candidate for the Archer Award, a prize so prestigious we only give it out once every five years—if there's a worthy applicant," Mrs. Notley said. "Which Kaitlyn certainly is."

"Thank you," replied the pretty girl who'd just come in. She looked kinda shy about receiving the high praise.

"And should she win, not only will her own tuition for the rest of her time here be paid for, but she'll be also able to send her children to Radiance one day tuition-free. Alumni connections run deep here, McCutcheon. We're what you might call a well-endowed institution with a highly motivated base of support for our objectives."

"*Pugnare ad consequi, consequi ad da.*" The girl said the words as if she'd repeated the phrase many times before. "It means..." she said, turning to me.

"'Fight to achieve, achieve to give,'" I said, finishing her sentence for her.

She paused. "You speak Latin?"

"No."

Her brow wrinkled.

"The engraving at the front of the school," I said. Apparently few visitors actually bothered to read it.

"Oh," she replied.

"Kaitlyn," Mrs. Notley said. "McCutcheon is considering a variety of educational opportunities next year, but it is my profound hope that Radiance will be his ultimate choice. Would you mind giving him Part One of the tour, please?"

"Yes, Mrs. Notley." Kaitlyn turned to me. "Welcome to Radiance." Our eyes met. Hers bright with intelligence, spirit, and life. Mine dark, deep, and full of secrets. "If you'll please follow me."

I rose and smoothed out my jeans.

"Lead the way."

EIGHT

On a scale from one to ten, the girl taking me on this tour posted an eleven. And that cute little schoolgirl uniform she wore was enough to turn the head of a blind man. Without a doubt Kaitlyn owned the whole package but, thing is, girls threw themselves at me all the time. What—did Mrs. Notley think that just because she could get one of her students to shake her ass a few times, I'd suddenly come running back to her office ready to give up my whole fight career for the chance to wear penny loafers to a wussy prep school?

What a freakin' joke.

"You have any ideas about which colleges you are going to apply to?" Kaitlyn asked me.

"Not really."

"Still undecided about a major?"

"Doubt I'm even going."

"No college?" she said. "Oh."

Kaitlyn walked us over to the engineering center where a few students were using artificial intelligence to create a robotics project.

"Impressive," I said.

Next she took me to see a drama class where some kids were restaging a scene from *Macbeth* as if Shakespeare had written the play in text messages.

"Impressive," I said.

"And this is our Alumni House," she told me as we paused at another stop on our tour. The place looked like a quaint cottage with little yellow flowers surrounding it and an old-fashioned metal mailbox out front. There was even a white picket fence.

"Immm-pressive," I said.

"Is something wrong?" Kaitlyn asked.

"Wrong?" I said. "Naw. It's just like, well, we got an alumni house where I go to school now, too."

"You do?"

"Uh huh," I replied. "It's called the penitentiary."

I smiled. She didn't.

"That was a joke," I said.

"Hysterical," she answered.

This whole school was so over-the-top I just wanted to laugh. Kaitlyn, however, remained polite.

"Would you like to see the new ecology project some of our students are currently working on?" she asked. "We're using renewable energy sources in an effort to be more green."

"Would that be before or after we sample the caviar being served for lunch?"

She put her hand firmly on her hip. "You think this whole place is a joke, don't you?"

"Not at all," I said with a grin that showed, yep, I did. Kaitlyn pushed back her hair and narrowed her blue-green eyes.

"Where do you go to school now?"

"Like you don't already know."

Her forehead wrinkled. "How would I know?" she said. "It's why I asked."

Though I didn't believe her because I was pretty sure that Mrs. Notley had already filled her in on my whole sad story, I humored her with an answer. "I go to Fenkell," I said. "Fenkell High, near East Seven Mile."

"Oh, I see," she replied as if a lightbulb had suddenly just gone off.

"What?" I asked. "What do you see?"

She chuckled in a now-I-get-it sort of way. "Hate to break it to you," Kaitlyn said, "but I do not for one minute feel like I have to apologize for the excellence of Radiance."

"Nope, you don't," I said. "Not at all."

There was a sarcastic bite to my response that provoked Kaitlyn into rolling her eyes. She chuckled a second time, but it wasn't a "ha-ha" type of laugh at all. "Let me tell you something," she said in a tone I'm sure she never used with Mrs. Notley. "Yes, this school offers a lot, but I know how hard I work and how much effort I put in to do well around here. I mean, I have absolutely no idea who you think you are, but trying to make me feel guilty? That is so lame. You don't know me. What are you, like some sort of stud football player?"

"Why can't I just be a regular ol' student?"

"That IS what I thought you were, a student," she answered. "Till a minute ago. Now I just think you're a, I don't know . . . a guy with a bad attitude."

"Naw," I said. "I ain't a football player."

We took a few steps in silence, each thinking about what next to say. Clearly, I'd gotten her all riled up because she started in on me again without my having yet said another word.

"Like I should really feel bad about all the opportunities I'm being given. Do you have any idea how hard I go at it to try to be the best? Up at the crack of dawn, living off of five hours of sleep every night just so I can try to make a few breaks for myself. What am I supposed to do, kick back and weep for all the kids who don't have the same chances I'm being given?"

Kaitlyn was aggravated. And the madder she got, the sexier I found her.

"Look, I don't wanna fight," I said in a calm and even voice. "Just answer me this."

"What?" she snipped.

I paused before posing my question. "So is that, like, a no on the caviar for lunch?"

I grinned, hoping she'd take the bait and lash out at me again, 'cause seeing her get all hot and bothered felt like it would be kinda entertaining. But her response surprised me, caught me totally off guard.

"Oh, do you feel sad? Do you feel hurt? I mean what's really going on with you, like deep down, to make you act like this?" she asked. "Wait, let me guess. Do you feel like a *viccccc-tim*?" She spoke in a high, whiny voice. "Oh, poor me, poor me, you don't know how tough I have it, poor, poor me?"

"Now you're goin' too far," I warned.

"What?" she said. "You can dish it out but you can't take it? *Psssh*. Figures."

"You don't know me," I snapped. "You don't know what the hell I'm going through."

"Funny, that sounds familiar."

We walked on in a tense silence. This girl had some nerve, I thought. I mean who did she think she was? This time it was me who finally said something straight out of the blue.

"All right, lemme ask you another question," I said to Kaitlyn, feeling aggro.

"Can't wait," she replied.

"If I do come to this school, do I have to wear a uniform?"

She rolled her eyes. "We all wear uniforms," she responded.

"And like," I asked, "do they come with the bitchy attitude or is that provided separate by the snob distribution center?"

She stopped in her tracks. "Tour's over, Mr. Cool Guy." Kaitlyn pointed west toward the sun. "Make a left at that building and it'll lead you back to Mrs. Notley's office."

"What, I don't get an escort?"

She walked off without responding.

"Love that skirt," I called out.

Without turning around she raised her middle finger. Classy, I thought.

I walked back to Mrs. Notley's ready to hightail it out of there. I wasn't ever gonna attend the University of Fantasyland, and while, sure, Kaitlyn was hot, hot, hot, chicks were a dime a dozen, and in a half hour I'd be back in my world and she'd stay in hers, the two of them forever separate.

Way I saw it, all these do-gooders who wanted to save a poor kid from the 'hood would have to find a different sucker to help them soothe their guilty consciences, or whatever they were doing. But hey, at least they could tell themselves that they'd *tried* to help the pitiful kid from the wrong side of the tracks who lived in the ghetto with no mom.

I entered Mrs. Notley's office and eyed the tall, brown grandfather clock sitting against the wall. I'd already missed a day of training for this nonsense, but ain't no way I was gonna risk not getting back in time to pick my sister up from Harriet Tubman.

"How was the tour?"

"I gotta be somewhere."

"That good, huh?" Mrs. Notley said.

I nudged my head toward the clock. Mrs. Notley's eyes followed mine, she checked the time, set down her pen, one of those fancy "writing instruments" that looked like it probably cost a coupla hundred dollars, and then she grabbed her purse and removed the keys to her shiny BMW.

"Where's Kaitlyn?" she asked.

"Dunno," I answered, and though I didn't say it, I really couldn't have given two shits if I ever saw that girl again.

NINE

Dad had me in the cage every week for the next month, out-of-towners coming in courtesy of the Priests to get a taste of the underground kid named Bam Bam who people knew was gonna one day own a belt. The more my rep grew, the more Sat Nite Fights I put in the W column, the more dollar bills my dad was able to put in his pocket.

And when you drink, gamble, snort speed, and bang hookers for a living, there ain't no such thing as having too many greenbacks in your jeans.

Seventy-two hours after a quick six-thousand-dollar payday, we were down to a half-empty ketchup bottle, some skim milk, and a jar of squeezable mayonnaise in the fridge. Clearly, the trickle-down theory wasn't trickling down. After my next fight, I knew I'd need to make sure that when payday came I'd score some extra cheese. Gem needed a new coat for the winter.

That's the thing about kids. They grow.

Only problem was to win my next purse I'd have to fight in a back-to-back round-robin and take home a victory in a two-wars-in-one-evening showdown. The Priests, always trying to make it more exciting, had set up an N-S-W-E elimination, so that to get paid, a fighter had to win two fights against two different warriors, instead of just one, kind of playoff-style like the Final Four of the NCAA basketball tournament.

Though Detroit is sorta in the East, I was selected to represent the West. Why? Who knew? None of the geniuses in the crowd probably even knew spit about geography anyway. All those folks cared about was coming out to get wasted, gamble, and witness destruction and the spilling of blood.

What the crowd ended up getting on N-S-W-E tourney night musta felt spine-tingling good. To be honest, something about that school visit had stuck in my gut and just sorta turned me raw. I'd been on a tear lately, just rippin' through dudes.

The hell with Radiance Academy, I thought. No matter how hard I tried, those words just kept rolling 'round and 'round though my head. *The hell with them.*

Straws were drawn. It'd be South vs. East and then North vs. West. To me, it didn't matter. I was always one of those fighters who'd take on all comers anyway. Just put a fool in front of me and ring the bell. The rest, I'd take care of on my own.

"Bam Bam, you feelin' good?" A fan rubbed my shoulders as I got ready to enter the cage.

"Yeah, you gonna bring it?" asked another.

I stared straight ahead, my eyes locked-in yet vacant, the expression of a cold-blooded assassin on my face. As always, I didn't say squat to the fans on my prefight march toward the cage.

"We love you, M.D.," a voice called out.

"Make us proud and fuck 'em up!"

I'd still not gotten comfortable with complete strangers touching me with their germy hands, paws that had been who the hell knew where before being placed on my body. And while I know these spectators didn't mean any harm, nowadays every time I walked to the cage I either got scratched by someone's fingernails or stabbed by the tip of a pen somebody was holding out as they tried to score an autograph.

"Bam Bam rules!"

"Fill me with your sperm, I wanna have your baby!!"

I blew through my first opponent in Round One with a heel strike to the face that split the guy's nose like a blacksmith's hammer smashing a grapefruit. Red face juice squirted high into the air and sprayed across the clean clothes of four onlookers in the front row who had cageside seats. Each of them jumped back in horror, upset that their outfits had been ruined, grossed out by being covered in the blood of a violent stranger.

Yet deep down, I knew they loved it, too. Beat the hell out of sitting in the cheap seats, didn't it?

After twenty-eight seconds, half my work in this crappy tournament was done.

"You left at least five hundred damn dollars on the table by not taking this to Round Three." My father's eyes were red and glassy. "Maybe more."

"Yes, sir."

"For the next fight," he poked his finger in my chest. "Round fuckin' Three. Got me?"

"Yes, sir."

My father squirted a bottle filled with high-electrolyte water into my mouth even though I didn't really need it. I'd actually broken more of a sweat warming up for the fight than I had fighting. "Go take a piss," he said to me. "We probably have at least thirty minutes before our next go."

Though I didn't have to whiz, I headed to the bathroom anyway. It was the only place in the whole venue where a fighter could have any privacy.

"Now this Dominican from Baltimore we got next," my father said as soon as I got back. He lit a menthol cigarette. "This mother fights dirty."

Everyone knows it's a free-for-all in underground cage fighting. "No holds barred" really does mean no holds barred, but that doesn't mean that there aren't a coupla unspoken rules.

No eyes, no biting, no nuts. In general, there's a "no orifice" rule, too: no putting your fingers in other fighter's holes. This means no fishhooking, eye-gouging, ear insertions, or jamming your fingers into open flesh wounds to try to tear a gash apart like a six-year-old ripping open a birthday present.

Straight out of the gate in fight number two, the Dominican went for my balls. Twice. Then he tried to thumb me in the eye.

"You better watch that dirty stuff."

"I eat your mother's tits."

The Dominican cracked a crooked smile that revealed broken front teeth and black, rotted gums.

"Dude, you need a dentist."

He smiled even bigger.

It wasn't too long before he launched a third nut shot with a low kick to the groin, and once again tried to thumb me in the eye.

"I'm warning you, man. Fight clean."

"Nipples," he said. "I chew them like candy bar."

He launched an elbow strike that missed, and I took the Dominican fighter to the ground. Once on the mat, he immediately tried to fishhook me by jamming his index finger two inches deep up my nostril.

One rip and my face would have been permanently disfigured.

I spun away and jumped to my feet. Wow, did I hate dirty fighters. Hell, I still had those half-moon teeth marks on my left triceps from where some Mohawk-haired fool had bitten me on the upper arm three years ago.

Screw it, I thought. It was time to teach someone a lesson.

I set up in a square wrestler's stance, exposing my face, guessing that he'd go for another cheap-shot eye gouge with his thumb. He did, but expecting the move, I snatched his arm and quickly ripped the Dominican into a savage wristlock. Making sure all the crowd could see, I held his hand up high in the air, then snapped his thumb backward in the opposite direction a thumb is supposed to go, using the full weight of my body to amplify the blow.

His tendon shredded like a piece of cheddar cheese. The crowd let out a groan. His joint split from the knuckle down past the wrist with a chilling *pop*, and I took a step backward so every spectator in the arena could get a clear look at the Dominican's mutilated hand. His thumb hung backward and limp like a tree branch torn from its roots by a hurricane. I'd ripped his tendon so far back the crowd could see his radial artery as the digit dangled in the wrong direction off his disfigured limb. It almost seemed like a fake Hollywood movie.

But this was real.

I heard gags. Then someone vomited. The Dominican collapsed to his knees. Hunched over, he dragged his wounded arm between his legs and, in his last coherent act, slapped the mat before I kicked him in the face like an NFL punter hammering a football sixty yards in the air downfield.

The Dominican hadn't just tapped out; with the move I'd just pulled on him, that guy would be lucky if he could ever hold a soupspoon again without using two hands.

The tourney was mine.

Cheers and boos flooded the arena as I walked to my corner. The cheers were for the violence; the boos because there wasn't enough of it. Both my fights had ended too quickly for the crowd's taste. Two short first-round wins meant that a lot of people would be heading home that night much earlier than they'd hoped.

My dad charged up to me. "I thought we said Round fuckin' Three?"

I didn't answer. Instead, my eyes drifted over to the Dominican lying sprawled on his back in the center of the cage.

He began to convulse.

"Hurry up," one of his team members cried out, rushing to his aid. "He's going into shock!"

At the sight of the frenzy to aid my fallen opponent, my dad cracked a smile. "That's my boy," he said, his anger fading. "The killa instinct, that's my mothafuckin' boy."

I spied Weasel about to approach, but before he caught up to me I took off. Just bolted. Hands slapped me and people shouted obscenities and fans of newly won money were waved in my face as I pushed my way through the crowd. Finally, I was able to disappear through a door in the back and enter the bathroom.

Where I could go throw up.

Inside the stall, I could still hear the cheers.

Bam Bam! Bam Bam!

Strands of yellow puke hung from my chin. My head spun like a whirling merry-go-round. My stomach, steel on the outside, soup on the inside, emptied into a toilet, where random pubic hairs dangled from the side of the bowl just inches from my face.

What was I becoming? I wondered to myself.

Suddenly, the door to the restroom slammed open.

"You throwing up? Are you throwing up? You gotta be fuckin' kidding me?"

I didn't respond. My dad kicked open the door to my stall.

"You are one soft son of a bitch, you know that? I should just put a skirt on you and check for a vagina." He smashed the stall's wall. "When you enter that cage you identify your opponent's weakness, you exploit it to maximum capacity, and then you force that motherfucker through unyielding anguish and pain to abandon all hope. Defense is offense, down is up, hurt is joy, and brutality is your best friend, so grow some big-boy nuts, son. A fighter who's not a monster is a fighter who ain't never gonna win a belt."

He grabbed me by my ear and pulled back my head.

"And one day, you're gonna be a world champ."

I pushed his arm away and spit into the toilet bowl. He glared from above, a look of disapproval and shame written all over his face.

"Get up," he finally said in a low, even voice. "Get up and go wash yourself off."

I rose from my knees, crossed to the sink, and turned on the water. Raising my eyes, I caught a glimpse of myself in the dirty, cracked mirror. A moment later I lowered my gaze, hating the sight I saw in front of me. The restroom door opened again.

"Great fights, kid. Great fights." Weasel entered with an unlit cigarette dangling from of his mouth and a second unlit cigarette stashed behind his ear. "Gotta nice, big delivery of green colored paper for ya after an evening like that. Woulda like to see it go a little longer, but hey, great fights, Bam Bam."

"What's the total?" my father asked.

"Seven large."

"Thought it was nine."

"You picked Round Three," Weasel responded. "Round Three, that shaved ya."

My father shot me a dirty look, reached for the envelope, and began to count the cash.

"It's all there, Demon. It's all there."

"Eat ass, Weasel," my father said as he double-checked to make sure every dollar he felt was owed to him had been placed into that envelope.

"Punk coulda detached your retina," Weasel said to me trying to make small talk while we waited for my father to finish counting the cash. "Make a fella blind with that low-rent, thumb-you-in-the-eye shit."

I spat into the sink.

"Serves him right what you did to that kid," Weasel said. "Serves him fuckin' right for messing with Bam Bam."

"He okay?" I asked.

"Who gives a piss if he's okay?" my father snapped. "We're square, Weasel. Now get lost."

"Of course we're square. Priests don't cheat, Priests don't cheat."

"I said go," my father repeated as he peeled me off three hundred dollars.

"I need at least eight."

Both my dad and Weasel froze.

"At least eight," I repeated.

Slowly, Weasel's head rotated over to turn and look at my father, the unlit cigarette still dangling from his lips. Both of us wondered the same thing: what was my dad's reaction going to be?

For a moment he was quiet. Still. Thoughtful. Then patiently, he reached into his pocket, withdrew a rectangular green package, a lighter, and then torched the end of a fresh menthol cigarette. A small waft of smoke rose from its tip and drifted into my father's eye, causing him to squint as he responded.

"Take a grand," he said to me as he peeled me off seven more crisp hundred-dollar bills. "'Cause see, that's what families do for one another, son."

Suddenly, I didn't want the money anymore. It felt dirty. He felt dirty. This whole damn thing felt smacked up and dirty.

I think my father sensed my sudden change of heart about wanting the cash, so he pressed it firmly into my hand and forced me to take it.

"Shit, there's more comin' from where this came from anyway, right, M.D.?" My father took a deep drag off of his cigarette and then courteously blew the smoke out the side of his mouth so as to not blow it in my face.

"Kid's a helluva fighter," Weasel said. "A helluva fuckin' fighter."

TEN

"So when I grow up I am going to write a book about a princess. But a princess that's a monster. And she likes cupcakes and unicorns and sparkles and when she waves her magic wand she can make as many kitty cats as she wants to appear but they all need to share the milk."

I walked Gemma to school on Monday morning, hand-in-hand as always, but as she chattered on, my mind felt a million miles away. It was inevitable that one day somebody was gonna catch me. Underground cage fighting with boys as badass as the ones I was starting to face was like riding a motorcycle in the rain at high speeds while weaving in and out of stop-'n'-go traffic. It wasn't a question of if I was gonna crash; only a matter of when.

No doubt I loved the sport of mixed martial arts. I loved the training. I loved the competition. I loved the hard and grueling challenges, too. The way it pushed me, tested me, hurt me, and dared me to fight back. But what I was doing lately had almost nothing to do with sport anymore. I was a whore, turning dirty, violent tricks for money.

And my dad was my pimp.

I used to feel pure on the inside, a man on a mission. A warrior. Nowadays, I don't know what I felt.

But whatever it was, it didn't feel good.

"Of course, the princess monster sparkle unicorn will love to keep eating cupcakes with vanilla frosting. The bottom can be chocolate or vanilla but the frosting has to be white because unicorns are white and that's how they get their magic powers."

We turned a corner and an icy wind whipped us. Gem's new purple coat, thick and long with a fluffy fur hood, kept her warm and toasty and did a good job of protecting her from the morning chill.

"Who's tough?"

"I'm tough."

"How tough?"

"So tough."

"And why are we tough?"

"'Cause that's the way we get out."

But was it? I thought. Were we really on our way out? Was there even a way for us to get out, or were we both trapped like rats in a cage, too stupid to know the game was rigged for us to lose all along?

"Gimme a kiss," I said shaking myself out of my daze, and she did. As usual, I waited until I saw Gem walk safely through the front door of her school before I turned and continued on to Fenkell.

"Hey, McCutcheon, got a sec?"

I rolled my eyes. I'd been on campus less than eight seconds, and already Mr. Freedman was handing me a packet.

"Some extra science material we'll never get to in class. You're gonna need it. Those kids at Radiance are much further along than we are."

Why the hell was he giving me this stuff? I never said I was gonna accept the offer. And he knew that. Man, I wish this guy would just leave me alone, I thought.

But not wanting to be rude, I took the materials.

"Thanks."

"No need to thank me, son," he answered. I skimmed the packet. Nothing jumped out as being too, too hard. "I do it because I care."

He nudged his head as if I should look to the left. I did and saw a gleaming blue BMW. The passenger-side window rolled down.

"Ready to go? There's more to see."

A droplet of rain, small and cool, hit me on the cheek.

"Don't tell me you're surprised?" Mrs. Notley said. "I told you, McCutcheon, I'm persnickety."

Mr. Freedman pulled a scarf from his coat pocket and wrapped it around his neck as a light drizzle began to fall.

"It's your ticket out, son," he said to me.

Mrs. Notley turned on her wipers. With a sleek hum they swept the light mist from her windshield.

"I imagine you already told the front office about this so those truancy officers don't hassle my pops?" I asked.

"All taken care of," Mr. Freedman assured me as he opened the car door so I could hop in. "Everything is long since taken care of."

Mr. Freedman's tone felt confident and sure. Almost

too confident and too sure, and for the first time I realized that maybe me "winning" that lottery might not have been so lucky and random after all. I mean, this was D-town, a city where practically every part of the government was crooked. Fixing a school lottery? Hell, Detroit's had mayors with hookers on the city payroll. When top peeps want something done around here, stuff gets done.

I climbed inside the car. The sweet smell of the leather hit my nose and my butt felt warm and toasty.

"Heaters in the seats," Mrs. Notley noted. "Kinda nice, no?"

Ass heaters? Only rich people would ever think of something like that.

"You'll have me back by noon?" I said.

She put the car in gear. "Yes."

I buckled my seat belt and we took off.

Driving down East Seven Mile in such a sweet car felt different than taking the bus or riding down the street in a hunk of junk. And though I woulda thought being in such an expensive vehicle would make me feel less safe, like we were a more obvious target for being carjacked or something, somehow, strangely, I felt better protected inside the BMW. Sorta insulated from the danger and dirtiness of the surroundings. The clean glass, the quiet hum of the powerful engine, it was like money bought folks a certain distance from the problems of the outside world.

Being in the Beemer changed my perceptions, too. Like on the bus, I never hardly noticed the crazy amount of churches we got on the streets around East Seven Mile, but as Mrs. Notley and I cruised through the neighborhood on the way to Radiance, I couldn't help but be amazed at how many damn different houses of worship there were around.

Churches, temples, cathedrals, ministries, on, and on. Spread between burned-out businesses, closed-down shops and long-ago abandoned retail stores, the cross of the savior felt like it was everywhere.

I started counting. Within three blocks I spotted five liquor stores and six churches. After another three blocks I counted two more liquor stores and four more churches. Selling booze or selling God seemed to be the only really money-makin' enterprises around these parts.

"What are you thinking about?" Mrs. Notley asked noticing that my mind seemed to be a million miles away.

"God," I replied.

"Do you believe in God?" she asked.

"Do you?"

"I do," she said and then she showed me the gold chain with the simple crucifix charm she wore around her neck. "Very much so."

"Me, well..." I said as we drove by yet another church. "Every night I say my prayers."

"But saying your prayers doesn't necessarily mean you believe," she said to me.

"I used to believe," I told her. "When I was a kid. Nowadays, I'm not sure. I mean when I look around and see all the hurt, all the pain, all the injustice, well...like I said, I'm not so sure."

I expected her to lecture me. To convince me. To spend

the rest of the car ride explaining to me why God existed, why God was good, why a person needed to believe in God and put God before everything else.

But she didn't. Instead, Mrs. Notley replied with a single word.

"Understandable," she said.

We didn't really talk about God any more the rest of the drive, but Mrs. Notley, with her simple one-word reply, had just done something I hadn't expected her to do.

She'd earned my respect.

■   ■   ■

Clearly, having to chaperone me around campus for a second time stood out as the highlight of Kaitlyn's day.

"And this is the library." Kaitlyn talked to me like she was speaking to a little kid. "See those things on the shelves? They are called b-o-o-o-o-ks."

"Oh, is that what they are?" I answered. "I wasn't sure, 'cause I do most of my reading on a tablet. But that printed stuff is quaint."

She scowled.

"And this campus is Wi-Fi, right? I mean I don't want to attend a school where I get, like, patchy Internet service." I grinned, big and wide.

"*Pfft,*" she replied. We exited the library.

"So what grade are you in, anyway?" I asked as she led me to another part of school. Without a doubt this was the biggest campus I'd ever seen. Place looked like a college.

"Going into twelfth."

"You're gonna be a senior?"

"My mom pushed me forward a year when I was little."

"That's funny," I replied. "My mom held me back a year."

I paused to let her think it was because I was dumb.

"She was an early childhood education specialist and knew how all the latest research showed that the oldest kids in class usually end up outperforming the youngest by the time they all graduate." I hopped over a tree branch. "But I'm sure you're really smart and all to be considered for that Arm Hair Award."

"The Archer Award."

"Whatever."

It was true about my mom. When she first met my dad, she was a twenty-year-old cashier working in a health food store going to school at night. My dad, only twenty-one at the time himself, came in looking for some vitamin supplements just at the point in his boxing career when he was getting ready to make a serious run for the belt. That means he was clean, sober, ambitious, filled with dreams, and, though I still find it hard to imagine, charming.

They fell in love, she got pregnant, he went on a losing streak, and it all went downhill from there. I still remember the nights of being a little kid trying to bury my head underneath the pillow to drown out the sounds of their fighting. In the morning, of course, he'd always apologize for the bruises and the welts and tell my mom how much he loved her. I guess she always bought it, 'cause she stuck with him for years.

By the time I'd graduated kindergarten, my mom had graduated salutatorian, the second in her class from a school of education, and she started teaching full-time. When Gemma was born, I remember feeling scared all the love for me would be sucked out of her heart and she wouldn't want me anymore.

I was wrong. That didn't happen till a few years later.

Kaitlyn and I followed along a stone path and passed by a sign that said PLEASE KEEP OFF THE GRASS. It seemed as if all the students at Radiance respected the request, too, because there were no parts of the lawn that had been trampled over.

At Fenkell, the only grass we had at school was the kind people smoked.

"Hey, wait," I said. "If you were pushed up a year and I was held back a year, that means..." I did the math in my head. "We're both about the same..."

"Don't get any ideas," Kaitlyn said.

"Too late," I replied. "Already did."

We made eye contact. She gazed at me with the look of someone who wanted to break the lock between our eyes but couldn't help from continuing to stare at me. I felt the same way. Though I didn't want to admit it, I'd been thinking about this girl every day since my last visit to campus. I didn't mean to. I'd tried all sorts of things to get her out of my head, but there was something about her that was different. Something that was strong and confident and intellectual and attractive.

Plus, I had to admit, the first time she and I met, I was

a total jerk. Really, she hadn't done anything to me, yet I acted like a punk. In a way, I kinda felt like I owed her an apology, but I was too scared to say anything to her about it.

Crazy, huh? I'll jump into a cage with bloodthirsty gorillas, not a shred of fear, but when it came to some little uniform-wearing prep school girl, a chick I'd only met one time and spent less than an hour with, I was intimidated. By what? I don't know. But I was nervous about something.

After a still moment in which the world around us melted away, Kaitlyn broke our eye contact and lowered her gaze. Trying to find something to say to quickly change the topic, she began blabbing on about some other features of the school.

"Over that way are the dorms. Radiance is a combination campus, part boarding school, part community resident. About thirty percent of our students actually live on the school's grounds. Do you want to see the living quarters?"

"Not really."

"Do you want to see the cafeteria?"

"Nope."

"Well, I, um, guess that ends today's tour."

"Too bad," I said.

"Why too bad?" she asked.

"'Cause," I replied. "It was just gettin' interesting."

ELEVEN

've got a bunch of memories of me and my mom sitting at the kitchen table when I was Gemma's age, reading, writing, working with jelly beans to learn math, and basically doing all kinds of stuff that was good for my brain.

They're good memories. They make me feel warm on the inside. But she picked up and ran off so fast that she'd left all her teaching stuff in the closet, so these days I use the materials to make sure Gem's brain doesn't turn into the kind of ghetto mush you see in the heads of so many of the knucklehead girls around our neighborhood.

Heck, my sister's way smarter than I ever was, anyway. Maybe one day she'll even win an Archer Award.

Yeah, right?

"And what's the hardest working muscle in the human body?" I asked as we stared at a picture of a skinless body, the bones, tissues, and organs were all colored-coded underneath the human skeleton in a book called *Anatomy for Kids*. Every Tuesday, come five p.m., before dinner and tub but after a snack, we concentrated on science.

"The heart," Gemma answered, pointing at the chest

cavity. "Because it has to pump all that blood through veins and vesselps and things."

"Vessels," I said, correcting her.

"Uh yeah, vessels. But like also, the heart never stops because if it does, a person will die, and then you'll be dead without breathing."

"You move your hands a lot when you speak," I said. "You know that?"

"I gesticulate."

"Excuse me?"

"That's what Miss Marsha said to me. She said I gesticulate and I articulate."

"Do you even know what those words mean?" I asked.

"Okay, gesticulate is like when you move your body a lot when you talk and articulate is when you like announce all the words with lots of clarifications and things."

Suddenly feeling inspired, Gemma popped out of her chair and began to dance, making up her own little song.

"I gesticulate and I articulate and the number eight is a cucumber gate." She wiggled her hips and held the pencil in her hand as if it were a microphone.

Her smiled beamed as she did a little hula-hula move. That smile was like a fireplace that kept my soul warm.

"Come here," I said. "I need to tickle you right now."

"Nooooo, Doc!" With an excited hoot, Gemma dashed off to the other side of the room, but I pounced like a leopard, snatched her up, and began to tickle her on the couch.

"Please, Doc, stop! I'm gonna pee."

We rolled around laughing and goofing, her singing

more lyrics about cucumber gates and bubble skates, whatever those were. Then, suddenly, we heard the sound of a key in the lock. The giggling stopped instantly. We both sat up a bit straighter as the front door opened.

"Gettin' ready to storm like a bitch out there."

My father, a half-smoked cigarette dangling from his lips, drops of rain on his black jacket, kicked the door to the apartment closed behind him, then crossed to the kitchen table and set down a brown paper bag on top of Gem's *Anatomy for Kids*. After getting himself a glass from the cupboard, he removed the contents of the bag. Though I'd never tasted cognac, I had to admit it came in a nice-looking bottle.

"Priests are gonna fly in even more fighters to face ya. Provin' real profitable for 'em with out-of-town talent." He parked himself in a chair at the end of the table and took a slow sip of his honey-colored drink. "Could be big fuckin' money in it for us. I'm trying to work it to get in closer with the Priests, maybe do a li'l somethin' somethin' with Weasel. Hookin' in with them, that's when the cash really starts to roll in."

Gemma waved her hand in front of her face. In our small apartment, it didn't take long for the secondhand smoke to drift over to the couch.

"You primed for this?" he asked me.

"O' course," I said scooping Gemma up. "Come on. Bath time." With my sister in my arms, I made my way to the bathroom, my father eyeballing me the whole way.

Neither Gem nor I ever knew when he'd be home. Or if

he'd be home. My father would just show up when he felt like it and leave when he felt like it, too.

I turned on the water for the tub and noticed that my dad had cranked his head around to watch us as I readied Gemma's bubble bath.

My sister peeled off her shirt. I reached out with my free hand and closed the bathroom door. A moment later, she was in the water.

I knew my father had no idea why I cared so much for my sister. He and I had discussed it many times before.

"A fella can't give a rat's ass about a female in this world, son, even if they are blood. Use 'em and toss 'em if they ain't got no good use no more, that's what my old man used to say to me, and he was right," he'd said. "I didn't listen to my old man and done had to learn that shit the hard way."

Though I'd never met him, my father's father was both an alcoholic and a heroin addict. He'd died young, stabbed in the chest with a pair of gardening scissors by the time he was forty-five, but not before he had tricked out his own daughter, my aunt, who I'd also never met. Forcing her into prostitution sounded insane to me, but, having been raised in Southeast Asia after his own father had fought in the Vietnam War, my grandfather learned to view women as disposable. Overseas, before he laid claim to his American passport and landed in Michigan, he'd watched poor people sell their kids, especially their girls but sometimes their boys, too, into the sex trade so that the family had cash to live on. That my grandfather had done the same to his own daughter here in America shocked the hell out of me, but my dad told me there's an underground market for all kinds of crazy stuff here in the United States for anyone who wants to open their eyes and see our country for what it really is.

"America likes to talk about apple pie and cheeseburgers 'n shit but we got some sick sum-bitches livin' in this land, and if the money is out there to buy it, ain't nothin' that ain't for sale. Even freaky-deaky sex with little kids."

After my father had finally realized he'd never hold a belt, never be a world champion, females simply became tools for him to be used as a man pleased in order to get whatever he wanted. He'd turned into his own dad. The only thing he never understood was why I viewed girls differently despite all his attempts to teach me otherwise.

Gemma splashed in the tub. Would I ever turn into my own dad? I wondered. Didn't seem possible, and yet the thought sent a chill up my spine.

"It's a wash hair night," I said to Gem.

"But, Doc, can't we..." her voice trailed off when she saw the fiery look in my eyes. I passed her the bottle of tearless shampoo, and without another word she took it. Gemma wasn't the best hair washer in the world, but she was learning and liked to do more and more things on her own, so I let her wash it herself while I went to clear the kitchen table and then start cooking dinner.

"You eating, too?" I asked.

"I live here, don't I?" my father answered. "What we havin'?"

"Chicken and broccoli."

"Make me some rice or a potato or something, too. Hey, Gemma?" my father suddenly called out, turning his head.

"Yeah?" she replied.

"Yeah? Is that how you talk to me? Yeah?"

"I mean, yes, sir?"

"Kid ain't got no manners," my father said to me as he took another sip of his cognac. "Hurry up in there," he cried out. "We only got one bathroom, and I gotta take a shit."

I closed the anatomy book sitting on the table, put away Gem's pencil box, and then spied the science packet Mr. Freedman had given me earlier in the day.

I lifted the materials and stared at them for a moment.

A college preparatory institution, huh?

I tossed the packet in the garbage and moved my kettle-bell by the wall to prepare for the nightly workout I'd be doing later.

The Radiance Academy. Ha fucking ha.

TWELVE

The next day I stepped out of the Emergency Exit Only door at the back of school, paying no attention to the sign that warned an alarm would sound if anyone opened the thing during school hours.

That alarm hadn't worked in years.

Once outside I thought about how much I preferred snow to cold, icy rain. Especially when the wind whips it sideways and it stings your skin like needles. Storms, when they hammer Detroit, pound with no mercy, and I could tell a big one was coming.

I pulled my hoodie tight, put my hands on the top silver rail, and got ready to jump over Fenkell's back fence.

"So now you're ditching my class?"

I turned but didn't answer.

"Mrs. Notley's been here three times these past two weeks," Mr. Freedman said. "There's still another visit."

"I ain't going to that school."

Mr. Freedman jammed his ungloved hands in his coat pockets to fight off the chill. "Brains trumps brawn in this world, son. And really, what's the income expectancy of a professional, um"—he looked at my swollen cheek—"skateboarder, anyway?"

"Very high," I told him. "When you make it to the top."

"You could break your neck," he answered. "Or should I say, 'have your neck broken for you'?"

Though I would have preferred to keep it entirely secret, almost all of the other students at Fenkell knew exactly what I did on Saturday nights. And kids talk. Fact is, with each new victory, the reputation of Bam Bam—only people who didn't really know me called me that—was growing into a local legend.

Funny, though, how no one actually has the power to stop underground cage fighting even though everyone knows it's going on. After all, it is illegal. But so is drug dealing, pimping, dogfighting, and so on. It's like all this stuff exists, and though pretty much the entire community is aware of it, no one does anything about it.

Maybe they just can't? Who's gonna stop it anyway, the cops? Hell, they don't rule these streets; they only hope to contain the chaos. It's gotten so bad 'round my 'hood that they don't even send in ambulances to help injured people without a police escort.

Even if someone is dying. A person could be lying there bleeding in the middle of the street, and unless there is a free cop car in the area, an ambulance won't even be dispatched if it's after the sun has set.

Naw, 'round here only one crew makes the laws of the land: the Priests. They rule without rival.

"Whereas becoming a doctor..." Mr. Freedman

continued, stamping his feet to keep warm. "With your knowledge of the human body, maybe you could heal people instead of hurt them."

I put my hands back on the top of the silver railing and got ready to jump the fence.

"I gotta go."

Time was ticking and gettin' to Loco'z early wouldn't hurt none. Nothing breaks routine.

"Let me ask you, son," Mr. Freedman said as he placed his hand on top of my arm as if he was going to stop me. "As a school official, am I really supposed to just let you jump the back fence of this campus right now and watch you leave?"

I looked up. Twenty-five yards away, three kids were jumping the fence in plain view. Ditching school was a tradition at Fenkell. At least seventy-five kids a day hopped the back fence, even more on testing days.

My eyes answered Mr. Freedman for me: *Who are you kiddin'?*

He gazed at me with the look of a man who wasn't angry. It was like he understood and even respected that I had my reasons for doing what I was doing, even though he didn't necessarily agree with them.

Mr. Freedman removed his hand from my arm. "Okay, go."

I readied to jump, but before I did he reached out and grabbed me again. "But just know that the only reason I'm even out here right now is because I care, son."

"Why?" I shot back. "Why do you care? Tell me. I'd really like to know. Why in the world do you care?"

With each word I spoke, frost blew out of my mouth like puffs of white smoke.

He responded, calm and even. "Come on back." He nudged his head toward the school building. "And I'll be happy to tell you."

With a strong push, I hoisted myself over.

"Another time," I said through the wire.

"Just remember," Mr. Freedman told me. "Everyone needs help at some point in their life, son. It's a rule without exception."

I gazed at him through the crisscrossed silver steel. "I help myself," I answered, and a moment later, I was gone.

■　　■　　■

"Need a ride?"

The weather had turned from bad to nasty with screaming winds, rain that slashed, and chunks of rock-hard hail starting to pelt us as darkness crept over the afternoon sky. Gemma and I could barely hear each other talk on our march home from school. Keeping our heads low and leaning forward into the gusts, we did our best to protect ourselves from the vicious weather. If I hadn't been holding her hand, I think the wind might have actually blown my sister off her feet and down the street like a cheap plastic bag caught in a wicked tornado.

"I said, need a ride?"

"Who's that?" Gemma asked in reference to the brown car that was riding along beside us.

"My science teacher."

"What's he doing? Did he follow you? His window's down and the inside of his car is getting all wet." Gemma's eyes were narrow, her face tight, and I could see small droplets of freezing cold water dripping from her eyelashes. "You know chinchillas like to . . ."

"Get in," I said, making a decision. I opened the door, hustled Gem out of the cold, and the two of us climbed inside the warm car.

Yeah, he'd followed me. And yeah, he wanted something, too.

"I'd like to invite you to dinner," he said to us as I closed the door.

Gemma waited for me to respond, knowing it wasn't her place to talk.

"So, whaddya like to eat, young lady?" Mr. Freedman asked with a smile aimed at my sister.

Gemma looked at me before answering. She knew not to speak to strangers, especially grown men, but since she was with me, she figured it was okay to respond.

"Meatballs."

"Meatballs? I love meatballs. Say, might you know anywhere that we can get some good and tasty ones?"

"Uh-huh." Gemma looked over at me again before answering, but I remained silent. "I know a place that serves the biggest, most delicious meatballs in all of anywhere."

"You *doooo*?" Mr. Freedman asked with an exaggerated tone.

"Yep, I sure do," Gemma answered, her voice growing more enthusiastic. "And if you have never had them then you are going to love, love, love them because they're big and they're round and when you put your fork in, juicy juices come out and *mmmm-mmm*, do you wanna go?"

"Well, you'll have to ask your brother," Mr. Freedman responded.

Gem looked at me with big, pleading eyes. "Can we take him there, Doc? Can we go to Spagatini's, please?"

Leverage. Mr. Freedman knew he had it, and I knew I didn't.

"Well, don't think I'm lettin' you off the hook for that third set of sight words later tonight."

"YAY, MEATBALLS!" Gemma exclaimed.

"On King Street, right?" he asked me.

I nodded. Gemma buckled her seat belt and smiled so wide, her lips stretched to the far ends of her face.

"Spagatini's," Mr. Freedman announced as he reached for his dashboard, adjusted a dial, and raised the heat in the car so we'd get warm more quickly. He and I made eye contact through the rearview mirror. "Here we come."

THIRTEEN

My sister and Mr. Freedman might be ordering meatballs in red sauce over thick spaghetti with a hunk of the house's special garlic bread on the side, but dinner for me consisted of only proteins and vegetables, none of them covered in salt or cooked in oil or butter.

"Strictly grilled," I said to our waitress. "No sauces or seasonings or anything, please."

"You got it." She made a note with a short green pencil, then scooped up the fourth place setting at our table since there were only going to be three of us. "Be right back with your drinks."

"Gonna be kinda bland," Mr. Freedman said to me as our waitress walked away.

"I don't eat for taste," I said. "I eat for energy."

I knew it would only be a matter of time before Gemma started staring at the machine with the clutch thingy where you could win a giant toy. And sure enough, not three minutes after we'd ordered, she looked at it longingly, then looked hopefully toward me. But she knew better than to ask. I only had twenty-five dollars in my pocket and I needed to score more whey powder for my protein shakes. Muscle recovery and endurance were far more important than stupid arcade games that had been rigged for players to lose anyway.

"So let me guess," Mr. Freedman said to my sister. "You're in, hmmm...tenth grade?"

"No," Gemma said with disbelief on her face that someone could think she was that old.

"Eleventh grade?"

"Noooo."

"Twelfth, you're a senior in high school?"

"No way, I'm only in kindergarten." Gemma rolled her eyes as if this man must be from outer space. "But I do like a boy who's in first grade only I think I might have to dump him because he picks his nose a lot."

Mr. Freedman laughed big and warm. "Oh, this one's a cutie," he said. "I mean adorable."

"Napkin on your lap, please," I told Gem as I helped her spread the white cloth over her thighs. "And not too much root beer," I added as the waitress brought our drinks.

"Your food'll be right up."

"Thank you," Mr. Freedman said.

Again, Gem looked longingly at the arcade machine. There must have been three hundred toys, some pink, some blue, some fluffy, most of it junk, behind its glass window. Her eyes turned to me and I shook my head no, but I tried to do it subtly so that Mr. Freedman wouldn't see. However, our red booth in Spagatini's wasn't the biggest space in the world, and Mr. Freedman caught on that my sister and I were having a back-and-forth silent exchange about something behind him.

He turned and looked over his shoulder where he saw the dumb arcade game. Lights flashed and blinked across the top of the machine as if to cry out WIN ME! WIN ME! Stupid thing was like crack cocaine for kids, sucking up people's hard-earned money for a high that lasted about three minutes...then you needed more.

In no time at all the waitress returned with our food. "I've got two orders of Spagatini's famous meatballs," she said, setting down a couple of plates that had been piled high. "And a grilled chicken and vegetable plate, no salt, no butter, no oil, no flavor." She set my dinner down. "Just teasin' honey."

"Thanks," I said.

Those meatballs didn't stand a chance against Gem. It was the best meal she'd been served in a long time, and she gobbled down each bite as if I hadn't fed her in a week.

"Food good?" Mr. Freedman asked.

"Mmm-hmmm," Gemma answered, her cheeks stuffed like a chipmunk.

"Slow down," I said. "It's not going anywhere."

Dinner was filled with a lot of chatter. Mr. Freedman knew how to talk to young kids, though—not all adults do—and Gemma opened up about her love of vanilla pudding, rainbows, and, of course, chinchillas. When she had no more room for even one more bite of meatballs, Gem looked at the machine, looked back up at me, and once again silently asked for a few bucks.

Though I still had half my food on my plate, the look on her face caused me to lose my appetite. Money was too tight to waste on a stupid arcade game that she had no chance of winning, but still, saying no to her always ripped my heart out. Gem deserved so much more than I could give her. But I had a fight on Saturday night and I needed my supplies to be fully prepared and at the top of my game, so all I could do was shake my head and feel guilty about having to say no.

"But I can do it," Gemma blurted out, breaking our silent conversation.

My eyes narrowed and I glared. She knew better than to speak out like that, especially in front of a stranger.

"Here you go, honey," Mr. Freedman said pulling a five-dollar bill out of his wallet. "Go get 'em."

He slid the money across the table.

"No!" I snapped. There were daggers in my eyes as I glared at Mr. Freedman. Then I softened. "I mean, no thank you," I added.

It was enough that I'd agreed that he could take us to dinner. But taking handouts? No way. We didn't do that from anybody.

"Really, it'd be my pleasure, son, and besides, it's only five bucks." Mr. Freedman waved the waitress over. "Heck, I spend at least that much on my latte and muffin every morning."

"Yes?" asked the waitress.

"Can this young lady please have five singles?" Mr. Freedman passed the five-spot to her.

"Sure. One sec."

"Who knows?" Mr. Freedman said to me. "She might even win."

"Some games are so rigged," I answered. "There's no way to win."

"And sometimes, son," he answered, "you just gotta believe."

The waitress brought back five singles and handed them to Mr. Freedman.

"Here you go, honey," he said as he passed the cash across the table to Gem. "Good luck."

She turned to me and paused, waiting for permission. Gemma knew not to take the money without my consent.

After a small moment of silence, I nodded. She instantly smiled, scooped up the money, and called out, "Thank you!" loud enough for the whole restaurant to hear. Watching Gemma so innocently and excitedly dash to the machine caused me to burn on the inside. No matter how much I did, no matter how many sacrifices I made, it never seemed to be enough. I mean, I couldn't even spring for a few stupid bucks for my kid sis to play a dumb arcade game. What kind of piece of shit older brother was I?

I wiped the side of my mouth with a napkin, ready to jam out of this place and get home already. Sometimes when I get like this, the only thing that can put out the fire burning inside of me is my kettlebell.

Mr. Freedman must have noticed my inner anger. "Really, it's not a big deal," he said.

"Why are you doing all this stuff for me?" I asked in an almost accusatory manner.

"Because I care."

"Why? I'm just a nothin' kid from the 'hood. There are thousands of us at Fenkell that no one gives a damn about."

"I was a nothing kid from the 'hood once, too," he answered. "A nothing kid who kinda liked science."

I glanced over to check on Gem. With her tongue out she worked the joystick of the arcade machine as bells jingled and lights flashed.

"Felt like all through high school I had to ignore taunts of 'teacher's pet' and so on," Mr. Freedman said. "I wasn't athletic like you, but eventually I earned myself an academic scholarship to a small college where I majored in chemistry. However, this was just when crack cocaine had started popping up, and some local drug dealers got the idea in their heads that Chemistry Boy needed to make crack for them."

Our waitress came by. "Coffee?"

Mr. Freedman nodded. "Yes, please." I waved my hand, no thank you.

"Of course, I refused," he continued. "And of course, they didn't like that, but making crack wasn't all that hard and the recipe was out there, so these thugs began cooking it up themselves. However, the head guy got this fool idea that since I was a chemist, I could invent another kind of drug for him that could be turned into a big moneymaker like crack. But I refused again."

"What happened?"

"They took my daughter hostage. And they said that if I didn't do like they told me, they'd kill her."

The waitress returned with the coffee. Mr. Freedman slowly stirred in some milk.

"So, like, what'd you do?" I asked.

"I was a graduate chemistry student. I didn't know how to invent narcotics, and they had my daughter. I did what any normal citizen would do. I called the FBI."

"They find her?" I asked.

"They did," Mr. Freedman answered. "Not alive, though."

His reply was so even, so entirely without emotion that immediately my heart sank, because I could tell the coolness of his reply was just a bullshit mask for the greatest hurt he'd ever suffered. Instinctively, I turned to check on Gem. She was still locked in on the arcade game, tongue wagging, standing on her tippy-toes, determined to conquer her longtime nemesis.

Though the milk had long since been mixed into his coffee, Mr. Freedman continued to stir his spoon in the hot drink. Of course I had questions, like a thousand of them, but I didn't press him for answers. Instead, I figured I'd let him continue when he was ready. He deserved at least that much, and if he decided that he didn't want to tell me any more, I'd accept it. Every last kid who goes to a school like Fenkell has a story about some fucked-up shit. Some you hear, most you don't. All of them have one thing in common though.

A hell of a lot of pain.

After a sip of his coffee, he went on.

"Believing in the power of the law, I told them I'd testify. The FBI was going to use me as a star witness to take down the Priests."

The Priests?

"They have deep roots here, son. Their power goes back, oh, a few decades."

Question after question started bubbling up, but I still didn't know if it was appropriate for me to ask anything. It just didn't feel right to pry even though I wanted to. Mr. Freedman, however, seemed to want to make a point about something, so he kept on talking.

"My wife, ya know, she left me. Blamed our daughter's death on me, thought I was an idiot for bringing in the FBI and she didn't want to go into Wit Sec. That's the Witness Protection Program where they change your name, identity, everything. But I *did* go into Wit Sec, and in a strange twist, I ended up joining the FBI in the Missing Persons department. I just never wanted another family to go through what I'd gone through. As a trained scientist, my skills transferred over pretty easily."

"So how'd you become a teacher?" I asked.

"Bureaucracy. Seventeen years of it. I'm a specialist in finding people who weren't meant to be found, yet I spent more time pushing paper than I did helping real citizens. Finally, I had enough and quit to do something meaningful."

"So you got a job at Fenkell?"

"My old high school. Name's not really Freedman, of course, but what happened was so many years ago that all those cats are either dead or in jail now anyway. The Priesthood goes on but individual Priests don't last all that long."

I turned again to double-check on Gemma. Everything was fine.

"Can I ask you a question?" I said.

"Sure."

"Are you happy being a teacher?"

"Naw," he said. "I'm disillusioned. Reaching kids who don't want to be reached—well...it's almost impossible." Mr. Freedman leaned forward. "But you, son. McCutcheon, you want to be reached."

He looked me deep in the eyes and for a moment, I felt as if he understood me. Better even than I understood myself. Of course I wanted to be reached. Who didn't? Who doesn't want someone to care for them, to think about them, to protect them from harm and to help them out when times get tough? My whole life was a brutal me-against-the-world battle, with the world having a lot more weapons in its arsenal than I had to fight back.

But those were the cards I was dealt, so instead of complaining, I just played them. Played 'em as best I could. Yet to think that suddenly some miracle was gonna occur where the Tooth Fairy magically popped out and put a life of ease and normalcy under my pillow, well...I was too old to believe in crap like that. Any break I'd get in this lifetime would be a break I'd have to make for myself. Miracles made for nice bedtime stories, but I lived on Planet Reality where the people were vicious—and they were cheaters and they were liars and they were thieves and they were thugs and the system everywhere was stacked entirely against fools who didn't keep their guard up at all times.

Basically, the world is hard. And to survive, you just gotta be harder.

Suddenly, Gemma screamed at the top of her lungs. I spun around, muscles clenched, ready to pounce.

"I DID IT!" she yelled.

She ran over to the booth. In her arms, a brand-new pink teddy bear. It was the biggest prize in the machine a player could win, and Gemma's smile beamed ear-to-ear.

"You see?" Mr. Freedman said to me as he nodded his head up and down in a knowing sort of way. "Sometimes, son, you just gotta believe."

■   ■   ■

By the time Mr. Freedman had pulled up in front of our building to drop us off at home, the storm had let up, and the sky, clear and crisp, shone with stars.

"Thank you," I said as I helped Gem climb out of the car. She clutched her pink teddy tight as if she'd never again let it go.

"Yeah, thank you very much," Gemma said. "Thank you for the meatballs and thank you for the root beer and thank you for the car ride when it was storming really bad and my eyeballs were freezing and thank you for the money and thank you for letting me play the game where I won Cuddles."

"Cuddles? Is that what you named your bear?" Mr. Freedman asked.

"Uh-huh. 'Cause he's the cuddliest and everyone needs a cuddle."

"Well, thank you for being such a delightful dinner guest," Mr. Freedman replied. "You were right. Those meatballs. The best ever."

"I also know where they make the best pancakes, too," Gemma added. "And waffles and bacon and buttered toast. Just in case you're ever hungry again for breakfast, that is."

"Okay, that's enough, Gem," I said.

"I was only offerin' in case he's ever hungry," she said to me. "'Cause he's a teacher and he goes to school every day and when you go to school without eating breakfast it makes your head fuzzy and it's hard to concentrate."

"Wait here a sec," I said to Gem as I put her on the curb and got ready to close the car door. But before I shut it and let Mr. Freedman drive away, I mentioned something to him that had kinda been on my mind.

"You know, if Mrs. Notley shows up again this week," I said, "perhaps, well...maybe I might be more findable."

Mr. Freedman smiled. "Have a nice evening, son."

I closed the door, and with a belly full of meatballs, he drove off.

FOURTEEN

At Loco'z I approached my training like a scientist. Efficient. Precise. A clear plan in hand that I'd always craft on the Sunday night before the beginning of each new week. Either I'd target certain muscle groups, focus on exact specific submission holds, or concentrate on improving my tactical defensive positions from a variety of angles. Making it up as I went was the enemy. Haphazard "just pull some random exercises out of my ass" gym days could lead to injuries or underdeveloped skill sets. Each activity built on every other activity, just like each brick built on every other brick when someone constructed a fortress. To achieve peak performance I had to avoid whim and make sure strategy ruled.

Always, this was my approach.

Except when my manager showed up.

On the afternoons when my dad popped in to train me—sometimes it would be three times in one week and sometimes it would be one time in three weeks—plans went out the window and he made me work on, well . . . whatever sort of jumped into his head.

"Let's go, combinations."

"Dad, I did stand-up striking yesterday."

"I know what I'm doing." He put on the focus mitts. "Now, burn those arms."

Nate-Neck and Klowner glanced over, lowered their gaze and then went back to work on their own regimens, minding their own business. Doing as I was told, I began throwing left-right-left punching combos.

"Got big stuff planned, M.D." My father always liked stepping onto the mat and guiding me through my workout. Reminded him of his old glory days. "Remember, rotate that shoulder and punch through the target."

My sweat broke into a lather, and after three minutes of right-left-rights, we mixed in ducking and counter hooks.

"Priests are settin' up a big payday. Gonna be a two-step process. Switch." I did as he ordered and flipped to a southpaw stance going through the routine from the top, starting with a right lead instead of a left. Being ambidextrous provided me more options for attack. I'd spent years teaching myself to strike from either side, left or right, with power, balance, and, most importantly, bad intentions from all angles.

"Next fight's against a bitch named Razor. They're flying him in from Oakland," my dad said. "California's got some monsters out there, and this guy's got a rep for being too, too nasty—but once you take him out, the Priests'll set up a huge dance against an undefeated fighter from New York named The Brooklyn Beast. Ever heard of him?"

"Who hasn't?"

"Switch again."

I jumped back into a traditional stance and struck the focus mitts with crisp, clear, lightning-fast shots.

"They say this Beast fight'll be a war for the ages, so big they're thinking about doing some kinda renegade live-stream, pay-per-view over the Internet, with a gambling book and all in order to let peeps coast-to-coast watch it."

"Dad, I wanna talk about..."

"The cheese'll be sweet for us," he continued. "Biggest we done ever made. Gotta say, I like the way these men be conceptualizing the future."

"You know, I was thinkin'...."

"And ain't no doubt, it's got me contemplating a new arrangement for us, too. Like me joining their organization, maybe becomin' a lieutenant or something with them. That shit would be a major step up."

"Dad, I wanna talk about school for a minute."

"Fuck school. You're a cage fighter."

I smashed the mitt.

"I CAN BE MORE THAN AN ANIMAL!"

The whole gym stopped, frozen by my outburst.

Every other fighter in Loco'z showed up to train by choice. They'd chosen this path for themselves. But me, I'd been forced into it before I even learned how to write my name in cursive, never thinking any other options might exist. Well, maybe I might want something else? Something different? Something that would spare me from ice bags and bruises and migraine headaches and constant bleeding, aches and pains. Anyone ever ask me that? Anyone?

No.

And who would dare deny me?

My own father, that's who. Thinks I'm his fucking slave.

"Education's for suckers," my dad said. "And rich kids. Naw. Ain't gonna be no school next year. You'll be droppin' out to train full-time just like we done planned, and once you're eighteen, *boom!* You're turnin' pro. Two years after that, maybe less, we'll be making that big-time endorsement cheese, 'cause you'll own the belt."

"Not my fuckin' belt! Little bitch jumps into the cage with me, it's gonna be night-night time." Seizure, hollering from across the gym, crossed his arms into his signature rear naked choke hold and began to shake, pretending to have an epileptic fit.

I ignored his trash talk and turned back to my dad.

"But I have an opportunity to..."

"That's right, you got an opportunity. An opportunity that very few people ever get in this lifetime, so quit being so goddamn selfish. You know how many friggin' sacrifices I've had to done make just for you to get to this point?"

I rolled my eyes. "*Psshh*," I muttered under my breath.

Not liking that one bit, my dad grabbed me by the jaw and cranked my head, forcing me to look straight ahead and face him.

"You can't change who you are, son. And that's my mothafucking blood running through your veins." He jammed his finger in my face. "That means you a fighter, got me?"

I didn't answer. *SMASH!* He slapped me across the face. Physically it hurt, but worse was the embarrassment. Every person in the gym, Klowner, Nate-Neck, even Loco saw him do it.

"I said, you got me?" he barked again.

"Yes, sir," I said meekly.

"Good, then let's get back to work." He raised the focus mitts and steadied his feet.

"Ha-ha, little boy got slapped by his daddy," Seizure clowned as he began to jump rope, a giant smile plastered across his face. "Boo-hoo, Boo-hoo!"

"You'z should talk a little less and focus on your own'z self a little more," Loco told him. "Like you'z is way behind on your dues."

"I'm good for it," Seizure answered.

"No money, I'll bounce ya," Loco warned. "This ain't a fookin' charity I am runnin' here. Scrape up some cash, Seizure, or you'z gone."

My dad clapped the mitts and showed me a target. "Let's go, combinations. One-two, one-two."

I went back to work on my right-left-rights with only one question remaining in my head.

I wonder what part of campus I'll be seeing tomorrow?

FIFTEEN

"Let me show you the PE facilities."

"Not the gym," I said with a grin as we entered through a set of double doors. "Around here it's called 'the facilities.'"

"We do offer a lot," Kaitlyn admitted. The hostility was gone from her voice, and though I doubt she would've said so, I sensed she was glad I was back.

I know I was.

"How many parts to this tour are there?" I asked.

"I guess as many as it takes to get you to say yes to coming here," Kaitlyn told me. "Mrs. Notley can be persnickety."

"I've heard that," I said.

"Inside this building, we've got a rock climbing wall, an indoor pool, racquetball courts..."

"Racquetball? Too bad. I prefer squash."

"What's the difference?" she asked.

"Tell you the truth, I have no idea."

We shared a laugh.

"And down there is the boys' locker room. I've never been in it, but if it's anything like the girls', there's individual shower stalls and a . . ."

"Hey, Kay," a voice cried out. "How'd you like to wash my butt?"

Kaitlyn and I spun around. Three big, athletic-looking guys, wearing nothing but towels as if they'd just gotten out of the shower, hollered at us from across the hall.

"Yeah, like apply a little lotion right here?"

One of the guys turned, raised his towel, and flashed the white of his rear end. The three of them laughed.

Kaitlyn didn't.

"What, is li'l Kay-Kay a prude? It's just my tush." A second guy raised his towel entirely, so that Kaitlyn got a full butt shot.

"Hey, guys, come on," I said. "Enough."

They hooted. "Enough? You mean enough of this?"

One of the guys nudged the other two, and a moment later we were looking at three bare-naked asses.

"I guess that's what they call a triple full moon," one of them yelled, and they chuckled and high-fived.

I glanced over at Kaitlyn. Her eyes were low and I could sense her shame. She was one of those rah-rah, school-loving kids who adored her campus, and the disrespect from these three dudes bothered her deeply.

I started walking toward them.

"I think you fellas oughta reconsider your behavior."

"Reconsider our behavior?" The three of them laughed

like they'd just been told the funniest joke they'd heard in a month. Suddenly, the tallest one's smile turned to a glare. "And who's gonna make us?"

"Yeah," said one of the other two as the three of them started walking toward me.

We met at the halfway point. I took a calm, even breath and stepped nose-to-nose with the leader of their pack. Surrounded by his friends on both my right and left, I issued a warning.

"I will give you once chance to reevaluate. My advice: take it."

I raised my eyes, daggers filled with threat and danger. Go to war long enough and you develop an air, an almost supernatural vibe that rises off of you like invisible steam just before combat. Other warriors understand it, they own the vibe too, but civilians, all they do is sense it.

And fear it tremendously.

To tell the truth, my guess was that I wouldn't even need to fight. I could tell I'd already climbed so deep inside their heads that it probably wouldn't be but moments before they backed down, their instincts for self-preservation taking over. Yes, it would be three on one; but no, the odds were not in their favor. Hell, these were suburban boys. With a simple glance I could see that each one had grown up with mommy wiping the cereal milk off their chin. True warriors learn to observe an instant truth when we look into an opponent's eyes, a truth about whether or not they have the heart for battle. None of these three had the balls to watch me turn one of their friends into a bleeding chunk of meat.

And most definitely, none of them had the skills to stop me from doing it, either. The only thing worse for any of them than witnessing me tear apart one of their buddies would to be on the receiving end themselves of my hurricanelike destruction should I decide to unleash a pain-filled, bloody, bone-snapping explosion.

For a moment it was silent, but the silence didn't last long.

"Come on guys," the tall one said. "Let's just, uh, go."

The three of them turned and wordlessly headed back inside the locker room, their wills broken with nothing more than a stare.

"I...um...I've never seen a...your eyes," Kaitlyn said. "They were like a wolf's."

"Just some skateboard intensity," I told her. "It's a look I give to competitors before I do a reverse ollie. Nothing to it, really."

"Nothing to it?"

"It's like Sun Tzu said: 'The best victory comes when one doesn't even have to fight.'"

"Sun who?"

"He was a kind of a famous skateboarder," I replied. Not sure she bought it, though.

Quiet, thoughtful, still puzzled, I could see that Kaitlyn was struggling to get her head wrapped around what she'd just seen. "Um, yeah, okay." Slowly we began walking toward another part of the campus.

Me, I was glad those fools backed down. For some reason I doubted it would have impressed Mrs. Notley all that much if, while on the tour, I'd put three of her students in an ambulance.

We started walking.

"Tell me something I don't know about you," Kaitlyn suddenly blurted out.

"Huh?"

"You heard me," she said as we strolled along the stone path that cut through the green grass. "Tell me something I don't know."

"What's to know?"

"A lot," she answered. "I bet you have a lot of secrets."

"Who, me? Nahhh."

"I seriously doubt that," Kaitlyn answered. "My gut tells me you've got a ton of surprises."

"Nope," I replied. "What you see is what you get."

We walked farther along. A bird chirped and then a squirrel scurried up a tree.

"You're different."

"Different than what?"

"Different from the other boys around here," she said. "I don't know how to explain it. They're just more, I don't know...transparent."

"Is that a good thing?" I asked.

"Not sure," she answered. "I'm still trying to figure it out."

"Well," I said. "Good luck with that."

Suddenly she stopped. "No offense, McCutcheon, but like that's exactly what I'm talking about. I mean I'm not sure this is gonna work if you're not willing to be more vulnerable."

"I'm never vulnerable."

"Oh."

Damn. I'd spit that out too quickly.

"Wait," I said. "What do you mean *'this'* ain't gonna work?"

"What?" Kaitlyn asked me. "You haven't been thinking that there might be a 'this'? Oh, I see," she added.

"See what? What are you talking about?"

"You already have a girlfriend," she answered.

I considered all the angles. Being vulnerable would be dangerous. Being vulnerable could lead to being hurt. Being vulnerable would lead to being emotional and emotions always clouded my thinking. After all, hooking up and getting down with a girl was one thing, but this, what I felt like when I was around her, well . . . I didn't know how to describe it.

It felt different. I mean, yeah, sure, most definitely I wanted to jump her bones, but also some other part of me simply wanted to hold her hand. Do something pleasant and nice and warm together like go on a picnic.

Yo, wake up, dude, I then said to myself. This girl's a princess, some Archer Award winner from a whole other planet. Really, what did we have in common? What could we ever talk about on a picnic? *Shee-it*, the last thing I needed right now in my life was a girl messing with my head. Letting Kaitlyn believe I had a girlfriend would give me the leverage I'd need to keep things status quo and roll right along.

I told myself to be strong, act smart, cut any ties before they became sticky knots that I couldn't undo. I had other things on my plate. Real things. More important things.

Big-time things.

Yep, I told myself, that'd be my plan. Just lie to her.

"Nope," I said. "Don't have a girlfriend."

Well, perhaps I was exaggerating the potential risks of everything.

She smiled. Something about the light in her eyes opened a locked door inside of me, and though I'd spent years reading the minds of opponents, it felt like the tables had just been turned, and Kaitlyn was suddenly able to read mine.

There was no defense against it, either. No counterattack. Though I could have had a hundred other girls, Kaitlyn was the first one I ever sensed I could fall for.

"So, are you going to tell me something?" she asked.

"On my fourteenth birthday I stopped by the market on my way home from school to buy three pink balloons."

I began a story I'd never told anyone before.

"You bought yourself three pink balloons for your own birthday?" she asked.

"Not for me, for my sister. We were born on the same day exactly eleven years apart."

"Wow, what are the odds of that?"

"Point-oh-oh-two-seven-four percent."

"You've done the math?"

"Those are the chances of two people being born on the

same day," I said. "One in three hundred and sixty-five. Converted to fractions, that's point-oh-oh-two-seven-four percent. Rounding up to include leap year, of course."

"Of course," Kaitlyn said, nodding. "Must make for memorable birthday parties at your house."

"My fourteenth was extra special. I'd gotten the balloons for Gemma figuring she's three, so I got three of 'em, right? But my mom, she beat me by a mile. Did a magic trick."

"A magic trick?"

"Yeah," I said. "She disappeared."

"I don't follow."

Staying on the path, we passed around the backside of the Alumni House as we made our way up toward the main administrative building again.

"Okay, picture this," I said. "I walk into my house carrying three pink balloons and am greeted by my father. He's smoking a cigarette. Says to me, 'Your mom's gone. She ain't coming back. Don't ever ask me about her again.' Then he took his cigarette and used the heat of the tip to pop two of the three balloons. 'Don't wanna spoil her,' he told me. ''Cause you and your sister are gonna have to start learnin' to do without.'"

"That's, wow . . . horrible," Kaitlyn said. "You must be so mad at your mom for leaving like that."

"Not really. I kinda like to imagine she's got a nice job, met a nice man, and is living in a nice, tall condominium building right now, just sorta waiting for the right day to come back and pick up her kids to take us all home."

"You really believe that?" Kaitlyn asked.

"No. But Gemma, my sister, does. She's only in kinder-garten, so she kinda needs to. But me," I said as I looked at the soft breeze blowing through the tall trees. "I've already seen too much of this world to believe in bullshit like that."

Just then Kaitlyn kissed me. She leaned forward and kissed me good, right on the lips. When our mouths parted I noticed her eyes were wet with tears.

I expect tears would have come to my eyes, too.

If I woulda let them.

"Don't ya think we ought to start heading back?" I said not looking at her.

"Yeah," she answered. "Guess we should."

Our footsteps were slow and casual, both of us sort of shuffling our feet more than we were actually walking. Across the way I spotted a gardener, his golf cart parked by a storage shed, trimming a hedge with a rusty pair of shears.

Of course they had gardeners, I thought to myself. Probably had pool men and valet parking attendants around here, too.

"Can I ask you something?" Kaitlyn said to me.

"Sure."

"Your mom, why'd she leave?"

"Don't know," I answered, but that was kind of a lie. I'd thought about it tons, considered why she'd left a million times. And every time I thought about it, I always came to the same conclusion.

She left because of me. It was my fault. When I was

twelve, thirteen years old, I'd rather fight than do home-work. I'd rather train than study. Nowadays, I've changed a hundred percent and I handle all of my business, but back then she used to have to nag and nag me to get my schoolwork done and do my chores, and probably she just got fed up with my never-ending crappy attitude.

I was a bad kid with bad dreams of MMA superstardom and she must have just gotten sick of it. Plus, a week before she left, she caught me starting to teach Gemma how to box a little bit—you can't ever begin too early—so I guess she figured to hell with these terrible kids and she took off to go live a happier life.

"Really, you don't know?" Kaitlyn asked me.

"Not really," I replied. "One day, though, I'm sure, I'll find out, but the thing is . . ." my voice trailed off.

"Thing is what?" she asked.

"Thing is," I said as nerves swirled in my gut, "I think I'm afraid to find out the real truth. Like maybe it's just better not to ever know?"

"Wow," Kaitlyn said.

"Wow what?" I asked.

"Wow," she answered. "You really are different."

I responded with a fake smile. On the inside, I wished she hadn't said that. Didn't she know that all I really wanted was to not be different, to be just the same as every other normal kid?

I'd always been different. Always been celebrated. Always been cheered. Always been told I'm one-of-a-kind.

Well, deep down I'd learned something about being different, something undeniably and horribly true.

Being different was lonely.

■   ■   ■

We walked past a large yellow construction truck, and I chuckled when I read the orange-and-black warning sign that said TEACHERS' PARKING LOT IS CLOSED. At Fenkell, we have roofs that leak right into our classrooms with teachers who use buckets sitting on school desks to prevent puddles; but over here, if there's a pothole the size of a nickel, they repave the entire faculty garage.

Lucky me, however, got an escort to Mrs. Notley's car, which had been parked down the hill on the main road. Something had come up, some headmaster stuff, so Kaitlyn kept me company for the ten or so minutes while I waited for my ride back to Fenkell.

Couldn't say I minded at all. After all, even a blind man would prefer to stare at Kaitlyn rather than Nate-Neck and his lopsided zigzag nose. As far as training went—well, I'd just make up for the missed time at Loco'z with some extra one-armed pushups at home later that night, I figured. No big deal.

"Sorry," Mrs. Notley said as she finally approached. "Never a dull moment around here."

"No worries," I told her as she pushed a button on her key chain and the doors to the BMW chirped open. "Your Archer winner's been keeping me good company."

"I haven't won yet," Kaitlyn said. "I think my chances are okay, but I still need to figure out the *conferre ad communitas* part of the application."

"The what?"

"*Conferre ad communitas*. It's Latin for *contribution to the community*. Not that there's anything wrong with saving the whales or fighting for clean water in Third World countries, but I want to figure out a way to make a different kind of difference, something unique yet sustainable and really has, you know, like a big impact on a person's life."

A horn, loud and deafening, suddenly honked.

"If you could just take a step back for us, please, ma'am," asked a big-bellied man wearing a white hard hat and neon yellow safety vest. Mrs. Notley, doing as she was asked, stepped a few feet to her left so that the giant construction truck reversing its way out of the school's main driveway had room to pass.

The big-bellied man stepped into the road, waved a stop sign, and halted traffic, the loud engine from the truck drowning out all the other sounds around us. Unable to get into the car or talk without screaming, the three of us watched and couldn't help but admire the truck driver's skill.

A moment later, the horn honked again as if the truck driver was saying "all clear" and good-bye to his big-bellied friend. Then traffic resumed.

That's when I noticed it—the green four-door parked across the street. It wasn't the car, however, that caused my muscles to tense and my fists to clench; it was the driver.

Weasel.

What was he doing here?

He and I made eye contact. Weasel slowly torched a cigarette, and then, confident I'd seen him, he turned on his ignition, put his car in gear, pulled into traffic, and drove away.

How long had he been watching me? I wondered. Clearly, he wanted me to see him—but why?

It didn't take me long to figure it all out. I was being sent a message, a message from my dad and a message from the Priests. Like property, I was owned, a valuable asset whose job it was to rake in profits. Eyes would be watching me. Always. Too many people were starting to make too much cash, and if anything risked interfering with the money flow, the business partners would have to step up and regulate.

"McCutcheon? Hey," Kaitlyn said trying to grab my attention. "Mrs. Notley, she's talking to you."

I woke from my daze.

"I said, are you ready?" Mrs. Notley asked.

"Um, yeah," I said, a bit hazy. "We better go."

I climbed into the BMW, and as we pulled away a new question suddenly entered my mind.

Was Kaitlyn now unsafe?

SIXTEEN

After picking Gemma up from school, we walked through the front door of the apartment, ready to jump straight into our usual routine.

But Dad was home. And he wasn't alone.

"Aw, he be kinda cute."

Gemma and I stared, frozen in our tracks.

Dad had brought a tall, chubby, dark-skinned lady home with him. She wore a blond wig, sparkly purple eye shadow, and a fluorescent blue skirt over white fishnet stockings that were torn at the knee. The dress, if it could be called that, allowed us to see more of her chest than was appropriate.

On her big chocolate boob I spied a large tattoo written in blue script.

Destiny

Immediately, I understood exactly what was going on. My dad had brought home a hooker.

For me.

"A man needs red meat," he said slapping the whore's butt as if to push her forward in a go-and-get-him type of way. "Dig in, son. Destiny here's got a magic about her. This woman is gonna turn you out!"

He laughed. My eyes narrowed, and I could feel my demeanor turning to ice. Though I tried to prevent any sign of the shock, shame, and repulsion I felt on the inside from appearing on my face, I was sure it was leaking out.

And in front of Gemma? I thought.

"No thanks."

"Huh?" my father said.

"Not interested," I told him.

"Wuuut?" the woman cried out, putting her hands on her hips. "Like I aint'z good enuff for ya? Baby, once you get a taste of me I..."

"Shut up!" my dad ordered. He pointed his finger at the woman's face, and his ferocious look sent her a clear message: *Keep your lip zipped unless you want to have it smashed.*

The hooker glared, but wisely, kept quiet.

"You gonna to be ready for this kid from Oakland on Saturday, or what?"

"I'll be ready."

"Funny how confident you are even though you've been missing trainin' to chase tail."

"I'll be ready," I repeated. Weasel had obviously reported back to him about Kaitlyn. My dad's solution: get me laid. "You ain't got to worry," I said, sickened by my father's thinking.

Gemma's eyes fixed straight ahead, mesmerized by this strange person in our living room.

"Take your jacket off, Gem," I told her. "And meet me in your room. We'll start your vocabulary words in there."

Gemma, hypnotized by sparkly purple eye shadow, didn't move.

"NOW!" I barked. She began to unzip her coat, and my father began to unzip his pants.

"Well, if you ain't gonna take her for a spin, I sure as shit will."

He nudged the woman toward the master bedroom, and without hesitation she went inside. Both Gem and I couldn't help but gawk as her bubble-shaped ass jiggled toward my father's bed.

"Ain't no good sense wastin' it," my father said to me. "Hell, she already done been paid for anyway."

He closed his door.

Wordlessly but hurrying, I went to Gemma's clock radio on the nightstand in her room, turned it on, and cranked up the volume as loud as the small machine could go. My hope was to drown out the sound of my dad having his way with a skanky hooker while Gemma and I attempted to study.

My father, however, was a loud man with a loud voice who liked to call out all kinds of nasty descriptions as he did what he did with the whore. Gemma kept looking at me with a puzzled expression.

"Just concentrate," I told her holding up another flash card. "Focus in and try to concentrate."

■ ■ ■

When my Saturday night fight rolled around, my father was nowhere to be found. Alone in my corner after the blood from the previous cage battle between two girls, one black and one brown, had been mopped off the mat, I looked across and saw Razor, my opponent, bouncing on his toes on the opposite side of the closed-in steel pen.

He glistened with prefight sweat, getting himself ready for war. His manager, a fat guy wearing a backward hat, massaged Razor's shoulders and inspired his fighter with fiery words about destruction and mayhem.

"You'll kick his teeth out!"

"Yeah!"

"You'll break his bones like plastic forks!"

"Yeah!"

"And if you get the chance," his manager squealed, veins practically popping out of his forehead, "snap his fucking neck!"

"FUCK YEAH!" Razor shouted. *"DEEEE-STRUCTION!!"*

Razor smashed himself in the face with two open handed slaps and roared like a lion. Lots of fighters take caffeine pills before big matches. Razor looked like he'd swallowed an entire espresso bar.

My eyes scanned the crowd. The fans buzzed, big and raucous. Sure, I might have been the hometown favorite, but I could tell a lot of people had made the trip out from California to cheer for their boy. His fans were vocal and hyped.

"Rip his flesh off, Razor."

"Gouge his fucking eyes out!"

Under the lights, Razor's skin shined eerily, and his swollen muscles rippled. Though twenty feet still separated us, I could already tell this was going to be a warrior's war.

Again, I looked out into the crowd. Still no Dad.

Me against the world, I thought as I took a slow, deep, breath to help me remain calm and focus on the task at hand. Though he and I had never met, I could tell Razor had been coached to hate me. And to hurt me badly if he got even the smallest window of opportunity.

I took another deep breath. *Me against the world.*

"How we feelin', M.D.? Ready to do this? Gotta find us some leverage tonight, Son, and apply it."

"Where the hell you been?"

"That how you talk to me?" my father said. I didn't answer. "I done had to arrange something," he continued. "Like securitizing our future, and shit."

"Well, jeez, Dad."

"Chill da fuck out and get your head straight," he told me. "Look, you know this bitch is gonna fight dirty tonight. See all that sweat?"

"Uh-huh."

"It ain't. It's body oil. Makes him slippery, impossible to grab. Total bullshit, but what you gonna do?" Dad reached into a black training bag. "Except this."

He flashed a bottle of baby oil.

"Two can play at that game."

I stared across the cage at Razor. Grappling with a

slicked up fighter was like trying to twist a doorknob with a hand greased in Vaseline. Any plans I had for straight wrestling just got shelved.

"No."

"What?"

"No," I said. "I ain't gonna cheat."

"But that mothafucker's cheating. We just evenin' the odds." My father squirted some oil in his hands and prepared to rub me down, but I pulled away.

"No," I said. "I ain't gonna do it."

"Center of the ring, gentlemen. It's go time."

Glaring at me, disgusted by my decision to fight with honor, my father threw the bottle of baby oil back inside the black bag and then kicked the thing for good measure. "Well, just make sure you watch his fingernails."

"Fingernails?"

"Why the fuck you think they call him Razor?"

The bell rang to begin the fight. Razor and I met in the center of the cage and started feeling one another out with strikes from the outside, neither of us really connecting with any shots of significance. Razor held a height advantage over me of about four inches, but I was thicker, with bigger traps and lats. Funny how he kind of looked like a giraffe, with a long neck, a pronounced Adam's apple, and bugged-out, googly eyes.

He attempted a sweeping roundhouse. I stepped inside, avoided the kick, and went for a takedown, but he slid right out of my grip.

Then he slashed me across the chest. It drew blood.

Those weren't fingernails on his hands; they were claws that had been filed into bladelike tips hardened with some kind of manicure gel. People in the crowd with bets placed on me booed when they saw the bloody scratches on my torso, but in a no-holds-barred cage fight, nobody is gonna DQ a fighter for cheating like this.

Because how can you break the rules when there aren't any? Last fighter standing wins. How he gets there just don't matter.

I struggled the entire first round, taking cut after cut. I wasn't fighting an MMA brawler; I was warring a greased-up wolverine. None of the wounds, however, would take me out—all they did was sting like hell—but walking back to my corner after the first part of our dance, I bled from a thousand small scrapes. After the first seven minutes of the match I definitely looked like the fight's big loser.

"M.D."

"What?"

"M.D.," my dad called out to me; but strangely, he was standing outside the cage instead of inside of it in my corner. "Over there," he said, pointing.

My eyes followed to where his finger directed me and suddenly, in the middle of a few hundred people, she and I made eye contact.

He brought her here?

Seeing me bloodied and sweaty, shirt off, in a cage, fighting a savage war in a savage place, she turned and headed for the exit.

"Kaitlyn!" I cried out.

But she kept going, and a minute later was gone. I spun around to face my father.

"Guess she didn't like the skateboarding," he said with a laugh as he torched a fresh cigarette and took a deep drag.

I lunged at him but the steel fence kept us separated.

"Aw, you're better off without her," he said. "Remember, bitches'll just slow a champ down."

I hardly even remember the rest of the fight aside from a few small things. Number one, the payout for the victory was eight thousand dollars. Also, Razor needed an emergency tracheotomy in order to breathe after my throat strike with a closed fist in Round Two collapsed his Adam's apple and caved in his larynx.

And those fans who'd made the trip out from Cali, well ...they didn't have much to say after that.

The most vivid image of the night, however, was the sight of the High Priest giving me a small nod of his head. He didn't take off his sunglasses. He didn't rise from his chair or cheer. The man didn't pump his fist or even clap his hands. But clearly, the evening's results were events of which he approved.

I walked home, about four miles, alone. Blood seeped through my T-shirt to my sweatshirt from all the scratches that had not yet closed. Something simple and true became clear to me as I stepped over a piece of rotted wood that lay in the middle of the dark, wet street.

I hated myself. And I completely hated what I'd become.

SEVENTEEN

Mrs. McCullough, my seventy-two-year-old neighbor who had white hair and couldn't hear a rhinoceros if it walked through our living room, always watched Gem for me on the Saturday nights when I fought. I didn't think she could do much if there was a fire, a burglar, or an accident of any sort, but I figured having someone there to stay with my sister while I was out would be better than having no one at all.

I turned the key and opened the door. Smoke rose from the tip of a menthol cigarette.

"Weasel's supps'd to pay me, not you."

I kicked the door shut behind me.

"I'm done," I said.

I couldn't tell by how much time my father had beaten me home, but Mrs. McCullough had already left and only about one-third of the bottle of cognac on the table next to him remained in the bottle.

"The hell you are," he responded coolly. "Next fight gonna be worth big-ass bucks."

"I'm done and I'm going to that school."

"That school...*ha*!" With a smirk he polished off the rest of the honey-colored liquor in his glass. "You can't run from your DNA, son. You don't belong at that school. You belong in a cage."

He took a long, deep, last drag off his cigarette before smashing out the butt in an ashtray. Then he stood.

"And as your father, you will do what I fucking say."

He approached, his hand out, like he was expecting something to be placed in it.

"My money. Give."

Yes, I had the envelope. But no, he wasn't touching it.

"You hear me?" he asked.

I didn't respond. He stepped closer.

"I said, do you hear me?"

He put his nose next to mine and narrowed his eyes.

"Son, you say, 'Yes, sir!' when I talk to you."

Again, I didn't respond, and he raised his hand to strike but I blocked the blow and then pointed my index finger at the center of his face.

"I said I'm done."

Anger flashed in his red, bloodshot eyes and he threw a crisp left hook, but I slipped the shot and charged for the inside. Since boxers like to box, I took him to the ground with a harai goshi, a hip sweep from judo that uses the momentum of your opponent against him.

His legs knocked over a lamp as he sailed ass-over-elbow through the air, and I slammed him to the floor. The cognac bottle flew across the room and shattered against the wall while my father crashed through a side table, the weight of his body blasting apart the cheap brown wood.

"Urrggh," he groaned.

Like a jungle cat I was on him. Elbow to the top of his head, knee to the kidney, a forearm shiver to the base of his jaw that landed clean and with the force of a thick metal pipe.

Triangle choke hold.

I locked him in a vicious figure-four that gave no options: no defense, no way to counterattack, no air to breathe.

The student had become the teacher.

Rage consumed me. Hate boiled. I began to squeeze and squeeze and squeeze.

I'd feared him for so long but now, going toe-to-toe, I realized I had nothing left to fear. He couldn't hurt me. He was done hurting me.

I would never let him hurt me ever again.

I tightened my vise grip around his neck. There was nothing he could do, no way to break the hold, no way to cry for help, no way to tap out. As he gagged and gasped and squirmed like a fish flopping on the deck of a boat pulled straight from the sea, I thought how the world would be better off without him.

His face turned purple. His eyes began to bulge. Strangulation in real life isn't the same as in the movies, where people gently fall asleep like a baby being rocked in the strangler's arms. Strangulation is a brutal, violent, ugly thing to witness.

And Gemma was watching it all.

She stood by her bedroom door in a fluffy pink and yellow pair of jammies, the sound of our fight having woken her. I hadn't seen her come in, but there she was. We connected through a gaze. In my eyes, she saw venom; in hers, I saw fear.

Suddenly I realized that if she saw me strangle our father to death in the middle of the living room it would be a trauma from which she'd never recover. Some memories, after all, just can't be erased.

I released my grip. My father wheezed and desperately sucked for air, struggling to catch his breath.

"I'm done," I said.

He rubbed his neck, rose to his feet, and made his way for the door.

"The hell you are," he said in a raspy voice.

The door opened, then closed and a moment later he was gone. An eerie quiet filled the apartment.

"Doc," my sister asked, too scared to even move. "Are you okay?"

I opened my arms. Gemma raced over to me, and I wrapped her in a big, safe hug.

"Don't cry," I said, squeezing her tight. "It's over. It's all over."

Of course, as soon as the door had shut behind him, I knew I'd just violated one of my father's golden rules.

Always finish your opponent.

"Ssshh, don't cry," I repeated. "It's gonna be okay. Ssshh."

EIGHTEEN

The bell to dismiss fourth period rang, and kids began to file out of class into the loud, chaotic, overcrowded halls.

"Hey, McCutcheon, gotta sec?"

Mr. Freedman spun around in his chair and then reached into the filing cabinet behind his desk. "Here's a few more activities that I think'll help cement your knowledge of..." He tried to pass me a folder, but I didn't take it.

Mr. Freedman's arm hung in the air. Finally, after an awkward moment had passed, he set down the folder.

"What's on your mind, son?"

"Nothing."

"Well, clearly, it isn't science."

"I said, nothing."

He glanced toward the door and waited until the last of his students had left so he could speak with me in private. Once we were alone, he cleaned his eyeglasses with the bottom of his striped red tie, then leaned back in his chair like some sort of wise professor.

"You know that a real man recognizes when it's time to ask for help."

Nonresponsive, I stared out the window. Gray skies, light snow, bleakness everywhere, inside and out.

"You shouldn't feel any shame about seeking some assistance with your troubles, son."

"Help yourself, old man," I snapped. "You're the one who hates his fucking job, not me."

I stormed out of the classroom, headed for the back fence, and then jumped over the top in one easy leap.

But I wasn't heading to Loco'z; I was off to the bus stop.

After two transfers and a half-mile walk in biting, bitter wind, I arrived at the front steps of Radiance.

PUGNARE AD CONSEQUI, CONSEQUI AD DA FIGHT TO ACHIEVE, ACHIEVE TO GIVE

Whatever, I thought.

Once there, it took me about fifteen minutes to find which class Kaitlyn was in and where that was. Then I had to wait another ten minutes for the period to end. When the teacher finally dismissed all of the students, I ambushed her in the hall.

"Hey, do you, um, have a moment?"

"Don't you ever speak to me again."

"But you need to know that—"

"I said, never," she repeated. "I can't even begin to . . . I'm just . . . I'm sickened by the whole thing."

Kaitlyn pulled her arms to her sides as if touching me

would somehow contaminate her, and she walked away, no words to even say how she felt or to describe what she'd seen the other night.

"G'head, then. Leave!" Some of her classmates in the hall turned their heads to see what was going on. "What do you know about having to put food in a little kid's belly? What do you know about having to shop at donation centers for clothing? Go ahead, run back to your precious little Archer Award. What the hell do you know about having to survive, anyway?"

I could feel wetness coming to my eyes. I was pissed at Kaitlyn, pissed at her for rejecting me.

But could I really blame her?

Naw, it wasn't Kaitlyn who I was pissed at. Deep down, I was pissed at me.

I knew I shouldn't have opened up to her. I knew it was a mistake to become emotional, to become vulnerable, to care. Though I hated to admit it, damn if what my father had said wasn't true.

Relationships'll just fuck a man up.

"I thought you were different," I called out to Kaitlyn.

She stopped, turned, and then lasered in on me with her blue-green eyes.

"I thought you were different, too," she responded.

She walked away. I didn't go after her. Instead, I flew out of Radiance and began my half-mile trek back to the bus stop. The conversation between Kaitlyn and me, though short, kept swimming around and around through my head the entire way back to east-side D-town.

"I thought you were different."

"I thought you were different, too."

Two bus transfers later I cruised up to the front gate of Harriet Tubman Elementary School to pick Gem up, my head and heart still scrambled like a coupla farm-fresh eggs.

"She's gone."

"Whaddya mean, she's gone?" I said.

"Like I told you, gone," the lady at the front gate explained to me. "Her daddy done picked her up 'bout twenty minutes ago."

"What?!"

I raced home. There was no Gemma; only a note.

BEAT THE BROOKLYN BEAST
IF YOU WANNA SEE UR LIL' GEM AGAIN.
FATHER KNOWS BEST.
P.S. LEVERAGE, LEVERAGE, LEVERAGE.

NINETEEN

The weather report said a nor'easter was blowing in. A bad one. A storm that would attack with fury.

I didn't care. I had to find Gemma. Where? No idea. How? I had no clue.

But so what. Not finding her wasn't an option.

I grabbed my jacket, bolted out the door, and began to hunt the streets. Starting at the Honey Pot near Hoover Street made the most sense to me 'cause I knew the bar would always give my dad a line of credit for drinks when he was tapped for cash. Not needing to have to have any cheese in his pocket in order to get hammered made the Honey Pot one of his fave joints around.

I entered through a heavy door, waved away a fog of cigarette smoke, and scanned the room. Drunks, unemployed do-nothings, a few sad-looking hoochies, and a couple of bank-robbing–looking sons of bitches were scattered across bar stools and small round-topped tables. The door closed behind me. I could practically feel the negative energy ooze from the room. It wasn't a mystery why my dad liked this place so much. His kind of people.

I approached the bar. Next to a rectangular Bud Light mirror, a large white sign warned that according to state law no one under the age of twenty-one would be served any alcohol.

"What'll it be?" the bartender asked me, preparing to pour something.

My eyes darted around before answering and then I spoke in a semi-loud voice because I'd wanted more than just the bartender to hear me.

"I'm looking for Demon Daniels."

A crash of pool balls from the pool table behind me exploded through the room. It was a violent collision, and its timing seemed to me to be more than just a coincidence.

"He's my dad," I added.

People got stabbed for opening their mouths and asking the wrong questions in dumps like these. Mentioning that Demon was my father would at least save me from anyone thinking I was too outta line for making this kind of inquiry. Yet still, I shoulda known no one would be stupid enough to answer. Responding to questions from strangers was enough to make people think you were a snitch, and everyone knew the golden rule about squealers in these parts.

Snitches got stitches.

A large, offensive lineman–sized black guy with a full beard and a gold hoop earring lined up his next shot at the pool table. He wore a blue Detroit Pistons basketball jersey underneath a black leather jacket, and I'd have laid two-to-one odds he was packin'.

"Six ball, back pocket."

He tapped his pool cue on the table, and then he and the bartender made eye contact. No words were exchanged between them, because words weren't necessary.

Even if the bartender did know something, he wasn't gonna say shit to me. The big guy in the Detroit basketball jersey was simply reminding the bartender of the code that existed. A code of silence that was rarely, if ever, broken.

"You got any ID, kid?" the bartender asked me.

"I said I'm his son."

He pointed at the door. "Get the fuck out."

I didn't move and thought about what to do. Picking a bar fight when I wasn't even sure if anyone knew anything seemed like a low-percentage play. The downside was high—I could catch a beat-down, maybe even a bullet—and at best I'd get a lead, which could prove to be total bullshit anyway. The more I thought about it, the more I realized my dad wouldn't be fool enough to hide out at his favorite bar anyway. He was a scumbag, but he wasn't an idiot.

"Well, if you see him," I said, getting ready to leave, "tell him I'm looking for him."

"Suck a nut, kid."

I left the Honey Pot and went to check the abandoned dry cleaners past Lumpkin where they run dice games and dogfights.

Nothing.

After that I scoped out the check-cashing joint by Mount Elliot, where people go to get fake ID's and forge legal documents.

Nothing.

Then I hit up the Super Lottery Liquor Outlet near Shields Ave., Sammy's Tire Shop close to Mound Road, and the burger and burrito stand close to Conant Street that also sold dime bags of weed with your french fries if you knew how to ask for 'em.

I checked and checked and checked. Nothing, nothing, nothing.

Rain turned to sleet. Ice pellets stabbed me. The gusts blew at more than twenty-five miles an hour, and the darker it got outside, the harder the storm hit. Sidewalks soon turned to icy slicks.

In some parts of Detroit, the city salts the streets so that cars can drive and pedestrians can walk. In other parts, they just let people slip and fall on their ass.

It didn't take Einstein to figure out which part of D-town I should still focus my search on.

Screw it, I finally said to myself after walking through the back alley of a few side streets where trannies were known to perform oral sex for twenty-dollar bills. I crossed down Van Dyke.

M.D., dude, you gotta go do it.

I headed to the C-Star, the one place I'd hoped not to go.

Club Stardust on Mitchell Street was a dark bar with a reputation for being a place where the worst of the worst went to drink, smoke, fight, and fuck. At the C-Star, the bar's nickname, there was a garbage-filled alley in the back where customers who had beefs with one another were encouraged to go settle their differences as opposed to smashing up the inside of the "fine establishment." I knew this because when I was twelve my father had staged a few fights for me in that alley.

Fights I'd won, of course.

But I also knew that above the C-Star, up a switch-back flight of wooden steps, there was an empty storage room with an old blue mattress on the floor, a thin one with stains and little cushioning, designated as a place for customers to go do the nasty if they had a partner and got the urge.

The reason I knew this is because on that mattress is where I'd lost my virginity. She'd been sixteen. Name was Chantelle. Said she wanted to be my first because she liked the way I threw roundhouse kicks to people's heads.

A guy never forgets his first. Me, I kinda wish I could. There was no specialness. No emotion. No real human connection or feeling, and after we'd finished, a part of me wondered if I'd even been Chantelle's first lay of the day, because she seemed so experienced in taking off and putting on her panties.

I was just meat to her. My whole life, I've just been a piece of meat. Except to Gem. She was my only real relationship.

The thought of Gem reminded me why I'd come to this hellhole in the first place. I opened the door of the C-Star and walked in, chest up, ready to find what I needed.

And if I had to hurt someone to get the information I was looking for I would. Enough was enough.

Suddenly, a shottie was pointed at my head.

"Don't move, motherfucker!"

"Hands up!"

My eyes scanned the scene, and I saw three more hand-guns locked in on me. Cops were everywhere.

"This the guy?" a voice called out. "This Ghost Jones?"

A scared looking black lady, thin, about thirty years old, shaking with fear, shook her head side-to-side.

"Naw. Ain't him."

A thick-necked cop spun me around and muscled me up against the wall. "What the fuck you doin' here? Get your hands up."

After patting me down and finding no weapons I was hustled out the back door and out into the alley where all the fights usually took place. Obviously, I'd just wandered into some sort of sting operation filled with trigger-happy police officers.

"Now, get lost and keep your mouth shut," a short, wiry cop warned me. "Shouldn't a kid like you be in school anyway?"

For a second I thought about telling this police officer my story, telling them about my kidnapped sister and my piece-of-shit father and how there was a crime that needed immediate investigating.

But I pretty much knew they wouldn't have done jack other than have me waste a few hours down at a station house filling out a bunch of stupid forms. Man, I really do wish the police would function like they're supposed to and take back this city, but I also know wishes are for little kids. Adults go out and handle their own business.

I threw my hood over my head, ignored the cop's question, and walked off. Being that they had other things going on, the police didn't hassle me further.

I continued on without learning who the cops were seeking to ambush or why. I'd never heard of Ghost Jones. Wasn't curious about him either. Had my own situation to deal with.

The hours dragged on. I hunted for my father. I hunted for Willie the Weasel. I hunted for any member of the Priests who might possibly know something, anything, but nobody talked and barely anyone acknowledged me. My search kept turning up nothing. And the more I walked, the more I searched, the longer I looked and came up empty, the more my mind raced in terrifying directions.

What if Gemma was being raped?

What if she was being beaten and punched?

What if Gem had been handed over to a sadistic fiend who took joy in carving the lips off of her...?

Stop! McCutcheon, you gotta stop!

I knew I was only making things worse by imagining all kinds of horrible things happening to my sister, but my fears had taken on a life of their own. The longer I wandered and looked for and scrambled to come up with some sort of something without being able to discover even a single clue, the more ragged, desperate, and fearful I became.

I began to bargain with God. *Please, take me!*

No answer.

I imagined bargaining with my father. *I promise, I'll fight in the cage for a thousand years.*

But I couldn't find him. Maybe the reason he'd kept Gemma around for all these years was because he knew that she could always be his ace in the hole in case things ever became sketchy between me and him.

Wow, the son of a bitch had played me like an Xbox. I swore to myself if I ever saw him again, I'd tear his throat out.

I began to bargain with the devil. *I swear, you can have my soul.*

There was no price I wasn't willing to pay, but still, I got no response.

■　　■　　■

I wandered aimlessly for two days around the ugliest parts of an ugly city, all of my prayers going entirely unanswered.

"Yo, my man, whatchu want?"

A street hustler with gold teeth, a fur collar on his bulky jacket, and a thick gold chain with a diamond-studded Ferrari charm dangling from his neck waved me over.

"What you selling?" I asked, my brain frazzled and fried.

"You got money?"

"I have money."

"Then I can get whatever da fuck you need. You want white to snort, green to smoke, smack to shoot, Ferrari Frank can scratch your every itch."

"I'm looking for a young kid."

"Aw, you one of them, huh? Boy or girl?"

"Girl. She's a..."

"Gimme a sec," he said, and before I could finish my thought Ferrari Frank slipped inside a burned-out building that didn't even have a front door.

How stupid is this, I thought while waiting for him to return. The chances of finding a random hustler who might know where I could locate my sister were less than those of winning a three-hundred-million-dollar lottery. Yet I had to try something. I'd been walking for so long with no food, no sleep, no leads, no clues. And I was desperate. Besides, sometimes street players know things about things that can help lead to other things.

Or so I hoped.

A rat scurried across the entrance and nibbled at the carcass of a dead cat. This part of Detroit was a war zone, for people and animals alike. Outside of sting operations, police never showed up until after the shootings stopped, ambulances didn't arrive until after bodies were cold, and firefighters didn't jump into their trucks until after all the flames had died down and turned whatever had been burning into smoldering ashes. Try to be a superhero and help someone in this part of town, and a person could end up in the morgue.

'Round here, people kept to themselves. But a cat named Ferrari Frank, a guy who wore a gold chain with a diamond-studded Ferrari charm dangling on the outside of his winter coat, was gonna help me? What the hell was I thinking? I decided to return to prowling the icy streets.

"This whatchu lookin' for?"

I turned around and saw that Ferrari Frank had emerged from the building with a girl. She couldn't have been more than eleven.

"Forty bucks, you can fuck her any way you like."

He parted her hair and pulled it to two sides making it look like pigtails.

"Young, dat's what you want, right?"

"I'm not . . . uh . . . the girl I'm looking for is five," I said.

"Aw, you a freak like dat?" He smiled approvingly, rubbed his chin and thought for a minute. "For that, I'll be needin' like four hours."

"But you can get girls that young?" I asked.

"Boys, girls, you name it. This here D-town, mothafucker, and our menu is thick as a phone book."

He grinned, proud of his city's extensive offerings, and I unloaded on him with a right to the jaw and then a left to the kidney. After staggering him, I grabbed him by the hood of his jacket and yanked his head down into a rising knee smash that landed clean and smashed in his nasal cavity.

Dude was out cold before he hit the ground. The young girl he'd brought with him from inside the building stared in amazement at the red blood, which began to spill out from his face into the fresh white snow.

"Go home," I said.

She didn't move. Instead she just stared, gazing at me with large, white, innocent eyes.

"Go home," I repeated.

"Now why da fuck you do that?" she asked. "How's I s'pposed to handle my business now, you motherfucker?"

She swung at me with a wild right.

"Stupid-ass bitch," she yelled, trying to kick me in the shins.

With my left hand I pushed her away. Once a pimp turns a girl out, their mind gets all twisted and they start believing that their captor is really their savior. I knew it didn't matter what I said or did at that point; this girl was gone, too far gone to ever get back.

As I walked away she punched me in the back.

"Fucker!" she yelled.

Again, my mind began to race. *Would that be Gem one day?*

I needed to find her!!

I started to run, hoping to halt the sinister voices that had once again begun to fill my head with horrible, horrific, dark, and sadistic ideas. Racing crazily along the slippery streets I headed for the only place, the last place, I could think to go.

It was before dawn when I arrived, so I waited under the shelter of a small doorway. Shivering, soaking wet, I stamped my feet to stay warm. After the morning light broke through the evening sky and night became day, cars began to pull into the parking lot.

His was the third vehicle to enter.

"I need your help," I said as soon as he opened the car door. Mr. Freedman raised his eyes, surprised to see me.

I knew I looked deranged. I hadn't slept, showered, eaten, or even sat down in almost seventy-two hours. Worst was the tears. They streamed down my face in uncontrollable waves, Niagara Falls.

"I need," I repeated, "your help."

A clap of thunder crashed in the sky. Mr. Freedman nodded.

"Of course, son," he said. "Of course, I'll help."

TWENTY

I took a seat in the tan folding chair Mr. Freedman kept by the side of his desk. In a simple, direct, all-business tone, he asked me for three things.

"Number one," he said. "Tell me everything."

I did. Held nothing back. I told him about Gemma. I told him about my father. I even told him everything I knew about the way the Priests operated their organization. I'd seen stuff over the years, stuff that no one in their right mind would ever dare talk about. But I was beyond caring. Let 'em shove a sawed-off shottie into my kidneys. Fuck 'em, I didn't care. Everything I knew about the High Priest, the drug network, the prostitution and extortion ring, the people who'd been murdered, I spilled.

"Number two," Mr. Freedman continued once he'd heard the entire story. "I'll need your trust."

I raised my eyes, a look of "no way" almost instinctively flashed across my face.

"You're gonna have to believe in me, son," he said. "Believe in what I say and in what I ask you to do."

He pushed a small bag across his desk. I peeked inside. Breakfast. His cinnamon roll.

Sugary junk food, I thought. Really?

Mr. Freedman nodded, signaling me to eat. I must have looked more in need of some nourishment than a stray three-legged dog.

I reached in the bag, picked off a chunk from the corner, trying to avoid the thick, white icing and plopped it in my mouth.

"Okay," I said chewing. "What else?"

"Number three, I want you to fight on Saturday night."

"What?"

"That's right," he said. "I want you to fight."

"The Brooklyn Beast? Tomorrow night?"

"Uh-huh," he said. "I fear you're gonna have to, son. It might be the only way we can smoke out all the players."

A fight tomorrow? I thought. Impossible. I was in absolutely no shape to pull it off, especially against a guy with a rep like this.

I took a deep breath. But if that's what needed to be done, I said to myself, then that's what I would do.

"All right," I told him. "I'll be there. You gonna come?"

"I will," he said. "As soon as I can get there. But let me ask you, do you have anyone you can get to be in your corner? You being alone for this doesn't make me happy at all. "

"I do," I said.

"Good, then contact them. And after that, go home and try to get some rest." He reached for his wallet. "And for

God's sake, get something to eat," he added as he passed me a twenty. "You look ragged, son."

I didn't take the cash. "I have money," I said, rising from my chair. "But thank you."

"Don't thank me yet, McCutcheon," Mr. Freedman said as he reached for his cell phone. "I'm going to do my best, son. Gonna call some people I haven't spoken to for quite some time, but don't thank me yet."

I wish I could have walked out of his classroom with a bit more hope in my heart than what he'd just left me with that last statement. I mean, it really would have been nice to leave Fenkell feeling as if it was all gonna be good.

But far from it was more likely. I left school with a rain cloud in my gut, but since I'd promised Mr. Freedman I'd put my faith in him and allow him to call the shots, I did what he'd said and scored myself a rotisserie chicken, an order of mixed vegetables, and a dry baked potato in order to try to give my body some much-needed fuel. After that, sleep.

Closing my eyes felt impossible, yet I was so exhausted I could barely stand. Only one thing seemed like it might be able to help me at that moment, so I did it.

I dropped to my knees and began to pray.

Whether God would deliver Gemma safely back to me, whether God even existed or heard me, I didn't know. But praying felt like I'd unloaded some kind of heavy burden from my heart. I prayed so hard I actually felt physically lighter. Even at ease.

Not peaceful, of course, but calm enough to at least finally fall asleep.

When I woke up it was Saturday, around noon. My first thought?

Only a few more hours till the fight.

■　■　■

I entered where I always did, through the broken back gates of the abandoned middle school on the west side of campus near the PE building, and scanned the arena.

It was still two hours before Fight Nite and the place was already buzzing unlike I'd ever seen it buzz before. The whole scene was nuts.

Suddenly, a poster caught my eye, an advertisement for tonight's fight that had been staple-gunned to the side of a telephone pole. I stared at the imagery.

BAM BAM vs. THE BROOKLYN BEAST
The Apocalyptic War

Someone had turned me into a cartoon, with muscles that hulked and blood that dripped from my mouth. I studied the picture and couldn't tell whether the red liquid flowing through my teeth was a result of me having taken a bunch of heavy shots to the face that I'd defiantly battled through or if the blood was from me having devoured an opponent, as if I were so vicious I had literally eaten chunks of his flesh.

The Brooklyn Beast looked like a prisoner from a super-max penitentiary, a monster of a man with the strength to rip off your arms and then beat you into a coma using your own limbs to batter and bloody you.

I narrowed my eyes and read the tagline at the bottom:

Mothers, hide your children!

I scoped out the crowd and saw hard, hard men in shiny suits, grandmothers who chain-smoked and cursed like construction workers, and young, hot women parading ballooning breasts the size of cantaloupes. I'd never seen the place so packed. Or the hordes so juiced. In fact, so many fans had shown up for the fight that the Priests had set up extra bleacher seats to accommodate everyone.

So this is what the big time feels like, I thought.

The energy that sizzled through the evening air, fueled by a cocktail of drugs and alcohol, felt electric. It was like everyone there was expecting a night to remember, and though the thought made my gut churn, I had a feeling, yeah, that no one would be disappointed.

To squeeze every dime out of the showdown, the Priests juiced the undercard matches with some unique twists: a deaf girl vs. a mute girl fight, a girl vs. a guy fight, a two girls vs. one guy fight, three traditional fights featuring up-and-comers and a "twins" super brawl where two sets of twin brothers would go at it at the same time, four in the cage fighting at once instead of just two. Truth is, it didn't seem to me that either set of "twins" were actually real-life brothers, but I doubt many in the crowd cared to verify their birth certificates. If someone got coldcocked and carried out on a stretcher, that'd be entertainment enough for the peeps in the audience.

Of course, Bam Bam was the main attraction. Not McCutcheon, not M.D., but Bam Bam. And he wasn't me. I felt like I was some sort of creature that had been manufactured in a toilet bowl of darkness. For some reason, I think I'd always imagined that success at this high of a level would feel different, that when the day came that I finally entered an arena like this as an undefeated cage warrior with screaming fans and electric hype, the "makes-your-blood-tingle" main attraction of the evening, it would feel good. Feel thrilling and awesome.

Instead, I just felt sick.

"Th-th-this guy, remember, you g-g-g-got the skills to take him, M.D." Nate-Neck rubbed my shoulders and tried to keep me loose. "F-f-f-fight your fight and fight s-s-s-smart."

"I never seen him dance myself," Klowner added. "But people I know say he's a wicked elbow striker with black belt level skills in BJJ."

Considering that there was no way my father was gonna do it, Nate-Neck and Klowner were cool enough to volunteer to be my cornermen for the evening, and while I found a small bit of comfort in their presence, the fact that Klowner wasn't cracking any jokes told me tons about what he was thinking.

I wasn't rested, I wasn't nourished, my head was a mess, and my eyes kept darting around as if I were looking for someone.

Which I was. I hadn't heard a peep from Mr. Freedman since I'd left his classroom yesterday, and though he promised he'd show, I still didn't see him anywhere.

I hungered for news. Any news. And then finally I got some, but it wasn't what I expected.

"Ain't no Beast."

"Huh?"

"Ain't no Beast."

I could see people scrambling to figure out what the whispers meant. Apparently, the Brooklyn Beast never made it. It wasn't that he wasn't in the arena; he wasn't even in Detroit.

A few techie guys adjusted the Web cameras that had been placed around the cage preparing for the upcoming live-stream broadcast. Despite the swirling rumors they continued on with their work making sure all the fight angles would be covered.

Finally, Willie the Weasel, pulling a cigarette from behind his ear, strutted up to me with a sideways walk to fill in the blanks. "Dipshit got 'rested last night for armed robbery in New York."

"So there's no match?" Klowner asked.

"Oh, gonna be a match. Gotta be a match, a good match, too." Weasel flipped open a lighter and torched the tip of his smoke. "People come to see Bam Bam, so Bam Bam they need to see."

I glared at Weasel, a burn in my eye. He could, I was sure, easily read my mind.

Where's my fucking sister?

Weasel squinted at me and then took a calm, self-confident drag off his smoke. Not only could he read my mind, but also, I could read his.

Touch a hair on my head and your li'l Gem will pay an ugly, ugly price.

Right then I swore to myself that if anything happened to her, I'd kill 'em all or die trying. That wasn't a threat; it was a personal promise.

"B-b-b-but who's he f-f-f-fighting?" Nate-Neck asked, steering the conversation back to the question at hand.

Weasel pointed across the arena.

"Him."

Klowner and Nate-Neck turned, then froze.

"No fucking way," Klowner blurted out.

I squinted into the lights.

"No fucking way."

Seizure.

Shirt off, sporting green and yellow trunks, the colors of Brazil, Seizure bounced into the cage grinning ear-to-ear.

He flexed his muscles, pointed at me, and then ripped his hand across his throat in a "slicing the jugular" move to rev up the crowd.

"One word, bitch," he yelled in my direction. Seizure crossed his arms into his signature rear naked choke hold and began to shake.

"Epileptic mothafucker!" he shouted. "Aayyy-aaaaagghhhh!"

The crowd exploded with delight. No they wouldn't be getting the Brooklyn Beast, but they'd still be getting the promised "Apocalyptic War" to decide once and for all who was the real pound-for-pound emperor of Detroit.

Seizure crossed the cage and jogged up to me. We stood face-to-face. "I been lookin' forward to dis for a long-ass time," he said with a fiendish smirk.

I didn't respond.

A fight with Seizure would violate one of the most highly respected unwritten rules in the world of MMA: guys who trained in the same gym almost never fought against each other outside of sparring.

"Th-th-there's a code, Seize, and you know it!" Nate-Neck yelled. "This is b-b-b-bullshit."

"Fuck da code," Seizure answered. "And if you want a piece of me, Neck, I'll straighten that crooked nose of yours and stick my dick in your ear when I'm done."

Nate-Neck leaped for the center of the cage, ready to go toe-to-toe, but Klowner jumped in front of Nate and held him back.

"Cool down, dude. Cool down."

Seizure smiled and stuck out his tongue like a punk kid you want to smash in the face with an ashtray.

"I'm right here N-N-N-N-Neck," Seizure said, mocking Nate's stutter.

"Composure, Nate," Klowner said. "Show some composure, buddy. Be the dignified man he ain't."

Nate-Neck cooled down, but I could tell he wanted a piece of Seizure more than a fat man on Weight Watchers wants a jelly doughnut.

I tried to figure out why Seizure would even take this fight. He was ranked number three in the world, and real pros like him were prohibited by the leagues from fighting on the underground circuit. But like a lot of knucklehead athletes, Seizure was a guy who would score a big payday and then blow it all on clubs, girls, clothes, cars, and living the high life. Clearly, he took this match because he needed the cheese.

But also, for Seizure it was a chance to settle once and for all who the real man of the city was. For months he'd been hearing the rumors, the innuendo, the disrespect to his reputation about Bam Bam being D-town's true chosen one, so tonight I knew he was coming to the ring with another thought in mind.

Total annihilation. It was time for him to bury the chatter in an unmarked grave.

Bury it for good.

With another smirk, Seizure backpedalled to his corner and again flashed his signature rear naked choke hold sign for the benefit of the crowd. Followed by another epileptic shake, of course. Half the mob roared with excitement; the others booed. This was the moment I realized that nothing less would do for him other than choking me out and sending me into a very public fit of involuntary, semiconscious convulsions for all the fight world to see.

Nate-Neck and Klowner spun around and hammered me with their outrage.

"It's not fair, M.D."

"It's h-h-h-horseshit."

I glanced to my left. Sitting cageside next to the High Priest in the chair usually reserved for the night's guest of honor was my father. Dressed in a pinstripe suit like an old-time Chicago gangster, he smiled at me and tipped his hat.

"Y-y-y-you don't have to f-f-f-fight him," Nate-Neck said. "You d-d-d-don't have to fight him at all."

But what Nate-Neck didn't know was, oh yes, I did.

TWENTY-ONE

When the bell rang to start Round One, Seizure shot out of his corner like a rocket, and though my brain told me to do one thing, my body did another. I was in the worst fight shape of the past few years and Seizure, like a fanged cobra sensing easy prey, pounced on me from the get-go. His onslaught of strikes, kicks, elbows, fists and knees were relentless, and within the first thirty seconds I'd been tagged with an assortment of big, clean, heavy shots that immediately put me in trouble.

Tired, weak from hunting the streets, emotionally drained from worrying about Gemma, all I could do was try to cover up and hold on.

Seizure, of course, was having none of it. Muay Thai is what they call the art of eight limbs. It felt like Seizure was assaulting me with sixteen.

I pushed forward, seeking a defensive clinch to shorten the distance between our bodies in order to slow his attack of blows, which were landing way too cleanly and with way too many good results for him, but Seizure was too big and too strong and too experienced and too determined and he continued to punish me with shots that hit me like bombs. I lurched forward. He nailed my forehead with a dirty boxing elbow that rattled my wits and blurred my vision, and then he threw me over the side of his body with a technically flawless hip sweep.

Suddenly, we were on the ground, and I found myself about to be snagged in a straight arm bar. At the forty-five-second mark Seizure was on the doorstep of owning me. If he got my elbow, I knew he'd snap it at the joint before I even had a chance to tap out.

Funny thing, however, about being in the cage is that only the warriors doing battle ever really know what's going on in a fight. From the outside, onlookers can speculate about the action. They can guess about the impact of factors like size, speed, degree of pain, and determination, but it's on the inside, and only on the inside, where the real truth of a cage war is known.

Yes, Seizure had me snagged. And yes, he would have cracked my elbow like an old wooden puppet. But as we grappled, I could tell his commitment to locking the arm bar wasn't quite one-hundred-percent, and a second later I found myself able to get my hips off the floor, turn my thumb toward my head, slide my knees up, and free my trapped arm by pushing inward toward his body. No, I couldn't get side control of Seizure as I executed the move, but I'd escaped, and a moment later we were both back on our feet.

Yes, I'd broken away.

To fans watching it probably looked like I'd pulled off a difficult escape. And I had. But also, I hadn't. Deep down I sensed that, though Seizure would have taken it, he didn't really want an arm bar.

Why?

Because he's a greedy motherfucker, that's why. He knew that a quick Round One submission against me could be easily dismissed. Fans could claim he'd just "gotten lucky." After all, anyone can get caught by a quick submission hold in a cage fight, so a Round One loss via a non-spectacular arm bar would have opened the door for all the Seizure haters to dump on his victory with claims that his win was nothing more than a fluke.

Seizure wanted total domination. It wasn't enough to just beat me; his plan was to destroy me. To eliminate me. To kick my ass and then choke me out for all the world to see.

That's why there was a lack of commitment for locking the arm bar; Seizure still wanted to administer more abuse. His plan was to have me lying in the center of the cage doing convulsions in front of the entire universe.

End of Bam Bam. End of story. The real king of Detroit cage fighting was named Seizure DeSilva . . . now, everyone go home.

The thought of it made a snapped elbow seem like a better tradeoff, but of course, Seizure wasn't offering options. All he was dishing out was punishment. To his way of thinking I'd exit the cage as a victim of his signature rear naked choke, and once he finally landed it, it'd be my night-night time, once and for all.

We traded strikes. We grappled. We intermixed judo with wrestling with Tae Kwan Do and we exchanged blow after blow, me on the receiving end much more than I was on the giving end. By time the first round ended, I felt as if I'd been beaten like an egg in a bowl. But at least I was still standing.

I staggered to my corner where both Nate-Neck and Klowner screamed at me to throw in the towel.

"This is crazy," Klowner said. "It's an outrage this fight is even happening."

"Y-y-y-you're in no shape for this, M.D. It's over. Be s-s-s-smart."

The two of them had been around mixed martial arts long enough to know the difference between a fighter who's simply taking some nasty shots and a fighter on the doorstep of being seriously hurt by his opponent.

"I'm t-t-t-tossing in the towel."

Nate-Neck raised a white rag that had been splotched with my blood, but I reached out and prevented his arm from completing the throw.

"No," I said.

Nate could have easily pushed my arm away and finished signaling my forfeit with a toss of the towel. But he didn't. Because there's another code between fellow cage warriors, another unspoken rule that says if a fighter has the heart to battle on, even if you don't think he should, it's his call to make, not yours.

"No," I repeated. Nate-Neck paused and thought about it long and hard. Then, against his better judgment, he lowered his arm.

"B-b-b-bullshit," he muttered.

Suddenly my father walked calmly and coolly up to the side of the cage.

"I got you down for a Round Three win tonight, son. We clear on where we stand?"

Anger boiled inside of me. Hate seethed. I wanted to climb out of the cage and rip his face off, but I knew that if I bailed out of this fight now and got into a scrum in the crowd, the Priests would separate us before I could do any real damage. And of course, that would open up the door to something very bad happening to Gem.

Assuming something already hadn't.

Don't think like that, McCutcheon. Stay positive and stay on task.

I took a long, slow, deep breath like I always did when I needed to calm myself, and then I ignored my father, lifted my eyes, and scanned the auditorium. *Where's Mr. Freedman?* I wondered. He still hadn't shown.

"Hey," my dad said, trying to snag my attention again. "Round Three, boy. There's a lot riding on this."

It went without saying that he was flying naked again. Probably super big-time, too.

"And by the way," he said to me with an evil smile. "I love the way you're making it look like you got no fuckin' chance. I got fools lining up to take my action right now."

My dad cackled as Klowner pressed an enswell against my eye to try to deal with the swelling of my face.

"Oh, and one word of advice," he said before walking away. "Leverage, leverage, leverage."

He returned to his seat next to the High Priest and flicked an imaginary piece of lint off his jacket. Asshole was acting as if dressed like this all the time.

"N-n-n-no need to be a h-h-h-hero, kid."

"Yeah, you don't have to do this," Klowner said.

But I did. I needed to find a way to win. However, when the bell rang for Round Two, it was more of the same.

Seizure beat on me like I was his personal human punching bag.

TWENTY-TWO

"**A**void the RNC. Whatever you do, avoid the RNC."

When fighters get cloudy after being rocked with too many shots, things get smaller and their outlook becomes less dimensional. They stop seeing angles, openings, and opportunities, and instead lock in on single, simple ideas that their jellied brains can still latch on to.

After Seizure tagged me with a spinning heel kick to the side of my head, this began happening to me, and all I kept telling myself was, "Avoid the RNC. Whatever you do, avoid the RNC."

The rear naked choke hold, Seizure's signature submission. I had to avoid it at all costs.

Seizure didn't want a heel hook, a knee bar, a kimura, or any other kind of compression lock. The only thing he wanted was an RNC so he could cut off the flow of blood to my brain. No matter what else he did to me, I promised myself I'd refuse to let him lock his elbow under my chin.

Round Two turned ugly and lopsided, and I took all sorts of big shots as a result of this "prevent an RNC at all costs" defensive strategy. Yes, our fight had found a rhythm, but I knew I couldn't sustain it. The bad part was, Seizure knew this, too. He was an experienced fighter, and patient, content to just whale away, picking and choosing his moments to strike, and whittle me down until the opportunity he most wanted opened up.

He tried three times for an RNC in Round Two, but each time I somehow managed to avoid getting caught. After I'd broken out of his third attempt and ended up in his half guard, Seizure smiled at me as if I were a puzzle he'd already figured out.

"Problem is," Seizure said, my blood speckled across his chest and shoulders, "you ain't tenderized enough yet."

He punched me in the face with a stinging left and then wagged his tongue, sensing I was running out of gas. And even if I wasn't running out of gas, he knew it was inevitable that at some point soon I would.

To his way of thinking, maybe the RNC he so desperately wanted would come in Round Four? Or Round Eight? Time, he knew, was on his side, so Seizure became content to toy with me and play it up for the crowd. He waggled his head then did a little Muhammad Ali–style windmill with his right before shuffling his feet. I felt like a mouse being dropped as food into the tank of a boa constrictor. Boas never strike when their food is served to them; they let the mouse sweat, get nervous, and worry. Only when the snake is ready to eat does it make its final move.

But once it does, the mouse gets devoured. Always.

My bottom lip bled, I'm sure he'd cracked one of my ribs, and there was a ringing in my left ear which wouldn't go away. Yet still I pressed on, jabbing, seeking safety in clinches, and most importantly, doing everything I could to avoid being trapped in a rear naked choke hold.

When the bell rang for the end of the second round every fan in the arena could see I was being destroyed. I even got the sense a few of my own die-hard fans felt bad for me. Watching their favorite fighter get chopped down and diced up was a hard, ugly, brutal thing.

"You're taking too much abuse," Klowner said as I sat in my corner.

"I can take more."

"But why would you?" he asked.

"Because I have to."

"B-b-b-be smart, M.D.," Nate-Neck said. "Walk away from this before you c-c-c-can't."

I thought carefully about my answer before responding. I hadn't told either of them about the situation with my sister because I didn't want to get them mixed up with the Priests in any way just for being associated with me. The less they knew, the better. And safer, I figured.

"What you guys don't realize is," I said to Nate-Neck and Klowner, "is that my strategy is actually working."

I took a deep drink from a bottle of high-electrolyte water as they thought about what I'd just told them. A moment later all three of us broke out in a laugh.

"This is your f-f-f-fuckin' strategy?"

"Oh, now it's the *kid* with all the jokes, huh?" Klowner said shaking his head. "Unbelievable."

Suddenly, Mr. Freedman appeared at the side of the cage and my eyes lit up.

"You find her?"

"This ain't television, son," he said. "When the FBI wants to find someone, they do."

"So that's a yes?" I asked.

"Uh-huh," he said. "That's a yes."

I could tell by his tone that she was safe, too, and my eyes began to swell with tears. Fact is, it felt as if a boulder had just been lifted off my chest, and I could actually breathe once again.

"Detroit just ain't that big of a city," he continued. "In fact, we found them both."

"Both?" I said.

"Yep, we found Gemma and we found your mother. They're out of harm's way now, son. And they're together."

My mother? Mr. Freedman must have seen the confused look on my face.

"She didn't run away, McCutcheon. He forced her to leave. Said he'd kill her if she got in the way of his championship lottery ticket. Literally, kill her."

I looked over at my dad. He held up three fingers for Round Three and then mouthed the word *NOW* to me.

"She never wanted him to use you like this, son," Mr. Freedman said as his eyes scanned the mayhem surrounding us. "And when she threatened to take you away, he threatened her life. Threatened Gemma's life, too. Not knowing what else to do, having no one to call for help, she just ran."

Klowner poured some water over the back of my neck and then wiped my face with a towel. I rose from my chair, feeling a newfound determination in my fists.

"It's over, McCutcheon," Mr. Freedman said. "Time to end this. You don't have to go back out there, son. It's all over."

My eyes narrowed and I shot a laser-beam stare across the cage at Seizure.

"Time to end this, indeed."

The bell rang to begin Round Three, and before Mr. Freedman or Klowner or Nate-Neck could say another word, I bolted into the center of the cage like a cheetah attacking a gazelle.

Bam-bam-bam! Three straight left-right-left combinations followed by a flying knee smash to Seizure's chest stunned him. He wasn't ready for a tornado to assault him at the top of the round, and for the first time in the match, Seizure was taking the big shots instead of delivering them.

I blistered him with a forearm shiver that caught him flush in the teeth and followed with a leg kick to the knee that landed with the ferociousness of a tire iron. Blood began to flow from Seizure's mouth, and the crowd erupted.

"Holy shit," yelled Weasel jumping to his feet. "Now we got a fucking fight!"

TWENTY-THREE

It was war. Back-'n-forth, back-'n-forth, back-'n-forth. Seizure was bigger than me, in better shape than I was, and also, he'd landed more shots, absorbed fewer blows, and had positioned himself so that almost any smart gambler would have been wise to pick him over me to eventually win the bout.

But Seizure would have had to be willing to die to take me out that night. And though he was a great fighter, he wasn't.

People call it lots of things. Guts. Heart. Balls. Whatever the word, it was my absolute refusal to back down that opened up the window I needed to find the fatal flaw in Seizure's defense. Having spied it, I rotated my shoulder and launched a missile, blistering him with the same straight right hand I'd hit him with six months ago back at Loco'z, the one that had nailed him right on the button.

My fist hit his chin with the force of everything I had in my tank, and Seizure went down.

"Get on him, M.D.," Klowner yelled. "Get on him!"

Seeing him stunned, eyes glazed, flat on his ass, I

pounced, and with four minutes gone in Round Three, I locked Seizure in a guillotine choke hold, one of MMA's most aggressive moves.

Tracheal compression is downright nasty. Makes your head spin. Makes your heart race. Sets off an internal panic alarm that can't be easily dealt with because it's instinctual, the fear of losing access to oxygen being part of our innate survival instincts.

Knowing I was right on the doorstep of the end of all this, I began to squeeze. No mercy.

The crowd went wild. Seizure desperately tried to bring his arm up and dig it between my body and my leg to break the guard, but I knew it would take an elephant gun to get me off of him now.

Nate-Neck and Klowner jumped in the air and banged on the side of the cage, exploding with excitement. People shot out of their chairs, craning their necks to see the turn of events. Everyone in the crowd stood, screamed, and strained to see the final climactic moments. I could feel Seizure begin to weaken. *Tap out* or *lights-out* would be his only options.

I yanked on Seizure's neck with every last fiber of strength I had inside of me. Then I saw my father.

No one was cheering louder. No one was more exhilarated. No one would benefit more from my victory.

"Finish that bitch, M.D.," he screamed. "Killa instinct time!!"

I paused and considered all the angles.

Then, a moment later, I slightly lifted my finger.

Not much, just sorta released my ring and pinkie finger, and though it might not sound like a lot, it was enough to give Seizure the ability to break my grip and dismantle the guillotine choke hold in which he'd been trapped.

Freed, he rolled away gasping for air, and a moment later we were once again on our feet, toe-to-toe.

My father's jaw dropped.

"WHAT DA FUCK ARE YOU DOING!?"

Yeah, I coulda ended it, but I realized that if I did end it then it would never end. At least for me, it wouldn't. With my dad now hooked in with the Priests and me now being the biggest draw on the circuit, would they ever really let me just walk away? Wouldn't they come after me again and again?

Would Gem ever really be safe?

No, only one way existed for me to get out from under their grip and get out for good. I knew exactly what had to be done.

Seventy-five seconds later I found myself snared in an RNC, a rear naked choke hold.

And Seizure began to squeeze.

I didn't tap. There was no point to tapping out. Seizure was gonna block the blood flow to my brain no matter what I did, regardless of whether I slapped the mat or not.

My father ran to the side of the cage, panicked. "What are you doing?" he screamed. "What are you doing, M.D.?"

My oxygen supply limited, the noise from the crowd

dimming, my head feeling lighter and lighter, I uttered a final, last phrase to my dad before Seizure completely turned out my lights.

"Applying leverage," I said.

He processed the information. My loss would mean my father would have to cover debts he had no way to pay, and the Priests certainly weren't going to listen to any of his jawing about how he was good for it.

Yep, it was lights-out for me, but that also meant it would be lights-out for Damien "Demon" Daniels, too.

A small smile came to my lips, and a moment later I lost consciousness.

TWENTY-FOUR

My eyes blinked open.

"It's over, son," Mr. Freedman said. "It's all over."

In a daze, I raised my head, looked down and saw my toes. Somebody had stretched me out on a table in the back locker room, where only the fighters and members of their team were permitted.

My body hurt all over. I was battered like I'd never been beaten before. But to my surprise, I was still alive. Had I suffered brain damage? I wasn't sure, but it didn't feel like it.

Nate-Neck and Klowner crowded around me.

"You got h-h-h-heart, kid. More heart than any f-f-f-fighter I ever seen."

"Personally, I woulda liked to see a Round Four," Klowner said. "I mean, in my opinion that fight coulda used a bit more action."

I smiled, but it hurt to laugh.

"I just have one question."

Not sure whose voice it was, I turned my head and saw

Seizure. He wore a white robe and held a blue ice bag up against a swollen left eye. His face puffed, he spoke softly.

"Why?" Seizure asked me.

I knew what he was talking about. Only we fighters inside the cage ever really know the truth about what goes on in a war. While not a soul in the arena knew I'd released my finger when I had Seizure trapped in the guillotine, he knew what I'd done and now he wanted to know why I didn't finish him off when I had my chance.

My guess was that this was the reason why Seizure didn't go all the way and send me into convulsions. To do so woulda broken the warrior's code.

I struggled to sit up.

"You're gonna be a world champ, Seize," I told him. "One day, you're gonna be the world champ."

He nodded. This was the end of the line for me when it came to cage fighting. I was still a kid, and kids, if they have any brains in their head, should go to school.

"Maybe I will be a world champ one day," Seizure said. "But pound for pound, we'll always know who was the best."

Seizure set down an envelope on the table beside me. Inside it were the night's winnings. Between the gigantic payout from the largest crowd ever assembled at the Sat Nite Fights and the extra side money Seizure had bet on himself to win, the total cash in the envelope he passed me came to seventy thousand dollars.

"That honor," he said, "will always belong to Bam Bam."

Seizure extended his arm. I wasn't sure if he could really afford to part with all the money he'd just given to me, but to mention anything about maybe me givin' him some of it back would have been a sign of disrespect. Seizure was a big boy, and I could tell it meant a lot to him to handle his business as he saw fit, like it was a way of being honorable and respecting the sport or something.

We slapped hands. Without another word Seizure walked out of the locker room, plans in his heart to train harder, work longer, become more disciplined, and one day win himself a belt.

■　　■　　■

I showered, changed clothes, and soon found myself alone with Mr. Freedman in his car. The first thing I did was ask how he'd found Gemma and my mom, but he didn't want to go there other than telling me, "I told you, son, I was FBI."

"Okay, but still," I said. "Like how do I know the Priests won't one day come after me again? Or Gem?"

"They won't," he said.

"But how do you know?"

"'Cause I struck a deal," he told me. "I told them I wouldn't get the Feds involved in any investigation of their activities like the drug dealing, gambling, extortion, or prostitution in exchange for a guarantee that they'd leave both you and your sister alone." Mr. Freedman scanned his eyes looking for a parking spot in midtown, but the streets were pretty busy. "Pretty simple when you think about it," he continued. "Makes no sense to risk an entire criminal enterprise over two measly kids, now does it?"

"And they agreed to this?" I said.

"Not at first. They wanted one more thing. Something I think they felt entitled to get whether we struck a deal or not."

"What?" I asked.

"Your father," he said to me. "You kids, they told me, would be free, but Demon, once they caught up with him, was theirs to do with as they wished. These terms, I was informed, were nonnegotiable."

Mr. Freedman suddenly spied a spot on Woodward, made an illegal U-turn, and began to angle his car into the open parking space.

"He snuck out of the arena in the chaos after the fight but with the way the Priests rule D-town, well . . . I suspect they've already caught up with him. I mean where could he possibly go?" He looked me in the eye. "I'm sorry for your loss, son."

My loss? Hmm, I'd have to think 'bout that. The idea that my father's life had already been taken didn't seem real. He was just here last night, and now today he wasn't? Just hard to get my head around it all at the moment. But like every kid who grows up round East Seven Mile, I'd heard lots of stories about how the Priests deal with folks stupid enough to cross them. Urban legends and stuff. With the Priests, it was never death by gunshot. Never death by stabbing or drowning, either. Dying was never quick. The Priests went for long, slow, drawn-out pain where the victim could feel, could see, could taste their life oozing away. Mr. Freedman seemed to think my dad was already dead, though I had a feeling he wasn't.

But soon would be.

"You got guts negotiating with them," I said.

"Aw, it's not so hard," he told me. "Not when you have leverage."

Having parked, Mr. Freedman unbuckled his seat belt and climbed out of the car. Me, I could hardly move. Butterflies the size of dragons fluttered in my stomach.

I looked up at the tall condominium. It seemed like the kind of place where everyone used the elevators and no one walked the stairs, a nice place to live, with air conditioning, maybe a fountain in the lobby.

I breathed in deep. It'd been years since I'd seen her, and the thought of now doing so had me scared.

I opened the door and dragged myself out of the car. Immediately I was smothered in a bear hug.

"My little Doc."

Mom was crying, yet she looked more beautiful than I remembered.

"God," she said as she looked to the heavens and squeezed me even tighter. "Thank you for answering my prayers."

■   ■   ■

Two weeks later Kaitlyn Cummings won the Archer Award. I was there to see it. We all were.

She iced it with the *conferre ad communitas*, the Latin part of her application that had asked about what her "contribution to the community" would be. Kaitlyn said, should the committee award her the prize, she'd transfer the entire scholarship to another student, keeping not a dime of it for herself. It would go to a younger kid who was only just beginning her education but someone who, with the help of a free ride to a top-tier school, would most certainly one day make, Kaitlyn felt, a great difference to the betterment of Detroit.

"Because one person at a time is the only way to change anything anyway," Kaitlyn had said.

And that's how Gemma became a student at Radiance.

"So, like, I get to go to this school with my brother?" she asked.

"Yep," Kaitlyn answered. "You and me both."

My heart melted.

"You look handsome, McCutcheon," Mrs. Notley said to me. "This uniform, if you don't mind me saying, fits you well."

Like a doting grandmother, she adjusted my collar.

"Thank you, Mrs. Notley."

"Of course." She removed her hand from my shirtsleeve, but I reached out and grabbed her by the wrist. Mrs. Notley paused, the strength of my grip surprising her.

"No, thank you," I repeated. "Thank you for being persnickety."

Her blue eyes lasered in on me.

"*Pugnare ad consequi, consequi ad da.*"

"'Fight to achieve,'" I said. "'And achieve to give.'"

"Exactly," she responded. "Then pass it on."

"You know," I told her, "I noticed that your science teacher was mighty pregnant the first time I was here. Perhaps when she pops, you might consider hiring this guy I know from my old school who always seems to have a file cabinet worth of extra-credit homework in his back pocket."

Mr. Freedman smiled.

"That's kind of you to say, McCutcheon, but I think I'm gonna stay where I am."

"Really," I said. "But think of the all the stuff you'd have here. All the possibilities, all the resources..."

"Yeah, it's true," Mr. Freedman said as his eyes scanned the campus. "This place does have a lot. But still, it lacks one thing."

"What's that?" I asked.

"Skateboarders," he said. "At Fenkell, I think we still might have a few more skateboarders in our halls. Don't you, son?"

I knew Mr. Freedman didn't necessarily mean cage fighters. He was just talking about any regular ol' kid who could use a caring adult to throw them a life raft as they battled through tough times. Sure, at Radiance there might be one or two students like this, but at Fenkell, the ocean was full of them.

"How can I ever pay you back?" I asked.

"Two ways, son," Mr. Freedman replied. "First, graduate. Detroit needs more kids with diplomas."

"For sure," I said. "What's number two?"

"Meatballs," he said. "You owe me some meatballs."

He extended his arm and I shook his hand like a man.

"Deal," I said.

"Okay, like, I have a question," Gemma interjected.

"What's that?" Kaitlyn asked.

"Do they have chinchillas here?"

"Excuse me?"

"You know," Gemma continued. "Chinchillas. 'Cause like I totally know what to feed them. See chinchillas need lots of exercise. When they are born they come out fully furred but as they grow, if their teeth don't get the proper things to eat, then they could run into all sorts of toothy issues that..."

I grabbed Gemma by the shoulders and spun her around.

"Who's tough?"

"I'm tough."

"How tough?"

"So tough."

"And why are we tough?" I asked, a steely look in my eye.

"'Cause that's the way we get out," she answered.

"Gimme a kiss," I said.

And she did.

TWENTY-FIVE

Everything was perfect. For three whole days, everything was like a dream.

Gemma was given a special "Welcome to Radiance" party by her new kindergarten teacher in order to help her feel more comfortable as a mid-year transfer. There were no chinchillas, but they did have a spiny-tailed green iguana as a class pet, which meant I got to hear the word "herbivore" about ten thousand times before the cycle of dinner, bath, book, prayers, and bed was completed.

When Gem locks in on something, she's like a pit bull. (And really, I've got no idea where she gets it from, either.)

Turns out my mom worked as the academic liaison for elementary school outreach for the Ford Motor Company, so she not only earned good money but she was home every night by five fifteen to make us a home-cooked, "sit down as a family" meal each evening. After tasting her garlic butter and Parmesan cheese mashed potatoes, I knew it wouldn't be too long before I got fat.

The condo was a three-bedroom, two-bath unit on the fourteenth floor of a well-kept building in downtown, and for the first time in my life, I had my own room. The bed was soft, the pillows were fluffy, and the covers were warm and toasty, but I decided to sleep on the floor. Maybe I'd get to the bed soon, I told myself, but for my first few nights, well...I guess I wasn't ready.

I didn't say anything to my mom though. Didn't want to worry her.

At Radiance I'd been placed in the science class of Mrs. Clascus just as they were about to start a second forensics unit revolving around arson, and though the P.E. coach really wanted me to join the wrestling team to help his squad climb out of the gutter in league standings, I took a pass and decided to give the chess team a go.

Mom had taught me a little chess back when I was a kid, but it turned out not to be enough. One-hundred-and-ten-pound weaklings were mopping the floor with my sorry butt. I didn't care, however, because I knew one day if I paid attention, worked hard, and learned from my mistakes, I'd get better.

Much better.

MMA is the sport of warriors. Chess is the sport of kings.

But best of all, I was finally able to walk through the halls with my head held high and a bounce in my step. It was as if I was floating.

And it wasn't because I thought I was some sort of badass who could take out any kid in the school, either.

It was because I had a girlfriend. My first.

And she meant more to me than the moon.

I literally found myself watching the classroom clock tick by like some sort of lovesick puppy counting the moments until I'd next see Kaitlyn. Holding hands in the halls, a kiss before I dropped her at class, a regular meeting scheduled at the top of the front steps by the entrance of the school after the last class of the day.

Like I said, the first seventy-two hours of my new life were perfect, and when the bell to end seventh-period English rang on Wednesday, I zipped out the door, the first kid in school to make it to the white steps, excited about what the future might hold.

Fear used to rule my heart. Nowadays fear had been replaced. With hope. It was all almost too good to be true.

I looked at the sign to my left.

PUGNARE AD CONSEQUI, CONSEQUI AD DA
FIGHT TO ACHIEVE, ACHIEVE TO GIVE

Without a doubt, Radiance was special.

At lunchtime Kaitlyn had mentioned she needed to stop by Mrs. Notley's office to do a thing or two for the Archer Award committee before we could meet up, grab a caramel latte from the campus coffee shop, and then head to the library together.

"Will you wait for me?" she asked.

"I've been waiting my whole life," I told her.

That response got me a big ol' kiss. I reached into my

backpack looking for my headphones, figuring I'd jam out to a few tunes while I waited for my girl.

"McCutcheon Daniels?"

I raised my eyes and saw a pair of thirty-something-year-old men walking up the white stairs toward me. Both stood about six feet, both had short haircuts, and both wore navy blue suits with white dress shirts and not-so-flashy black dress shoes. Only their ties—one wore green stripes, the other blue—were different.

"Who's asking?" I said.

"I'm Mr. A. This is Mr. B."

I chuckled. "Those your real names?"

"We'd like you to come with us, son."

"Am I under arrest?" I'd never seen two more white-bread guys in all my life. These dudes had to be some kind of cops.

"No, you are not under arrest."

"Then thanks but no thanks," I responded. "Don't think I can help you fellas out too much."

A person grows up where I did and they automatically learn how it's best to never talk to the law. Hardly nothing good ever comes of it.

I turned away hoping they'd get the message and leave.

"Do you happen to know a Nathan Thomas Wachowski?"

I paused. *Nate-Neck?*

"Or David Elbert Klowner?"

"Yeah," I said, turning back around. "What about 'em?"

Each of the two guys scanned the perimeter as if they wanted to make sure the coast was clear before continuing. Students had begun to flow out of the building, but kids didn't seem to be of any concern to them. After a moment, the guy in the blue tie continued.

"We're sorry to inform you," he began in a tone that showed no evidence at all of him being sorry about anything, "that both of their bodies were found this morning in an alley behind the Cooper Street Liquor Mart."

"They're dead," his partner said.

The man in the blue tie—I didn't know which of these guys was Mr. A or Mr. B—passed me a rectangular manila envelope and nodded as if I should open it and look inside.

I did.

Wish I hadn't.

I'd never seen police photos of a homicide before. Both Nate-Neck and Klowner were lying on top of one another like lifeless crash-test dummies that had been thoughtlessly tossed out of the back door of a shitty bar into a puddle of mud and garbage. Their faces were pummeled, their eye sockets puffed, and their eyeballs stared straight ahead, wide open yet not blinking, gazing at nothingness. I studied the picture more closely and noticed that Nate-Neck had a four-inch gash that ran diagonally from his eyebrow to his hairline, and his jaw looked like it was cockeyed, as if it wouldn't have lined up or something if you had tried to close his mouth.

Klowner was missing three teeth and a chunk of his right ear.

Most disturbing, however, were their throats. They'd been sliced at the jugular, gashed so deep and cut so thick that I could see the white of their spinal cords through the front of their slashed, bloodied necks. It takes a big knife to make a wound like that, I thought, a hunting knife or even a machete. And considering how badass both Klowner and Nate-Neck were, I couldn't even begin to imagine what kind of ferocious sons-a-bitches it must have taken to do this to them.

Klowner and Nate-Neck dead? The thought didn't add up. *But who? Why?*

"And we have reason to believe that you and your family are not safe," said the man in the blue tie.

My head snapped up from looking down at the gruesome pics.

"Gemma?" I said. "Where's Gemma?"

I spun around, eyeballed the campus, and began considering the direction in which I ought to race off in order to go and get her.

"She's in that white van," said the guy in the green tie as he pointed toward the street. "And your mother's in there, too." My eyes followed the direction in which he pointed, and sure enough, there was a white windowless van parked on the road by the front gate of school.

"Who the hell are you guys?"

"McCutcheon," said the man in blue. "It is our opinion that you should also enter the white van."

"I said who the hell are you?"

"We're United States Marshals from the Division of Witness Protection Services," the man in the green tie said. "As was mentioned a moment ago, you're not currently sa..."

Suddenly, without completing his sentence, the man in the green tie put his hand to his right ear, listened as if someone were speaking to him in a hidden earpiece, and raised his eyes. A moment later he spoke into his jacket collar as if he were wearing a concealed mike.

"Four o'clock, I see him." The guy in the blue tie stepped in front of me as if he was going to shield me from something that was about to happen, but I was having none of it and stepped to the side so I could defend myself.

Mr. Freedman bounded up the stairs.

"This is bullshit, Farmer! Total and complete bullshit," he yelled. "You think I wasn't going to find out about it?"

"Stand down, Freedman."

"The hell I will," Mr. Freedman answered as he arrived next to us. "We had a deal."

"Terms change," the guy in the green tie coolly replied. "You know that as well as anyone, Freedman. All deals can flip to no deal and vice versa."

"Bullshit," Mr. Freedman shot back. "I wanna talk to Stanzer."

"Stanzer's the one who pulled the trigger on this. Now, stand down, Freedman."

"What's bullshit?" I said interrupting. "What's going on?"

Mr. Freedman paused before answering me. His brow was wrinkled, his eyes were narrow, and I don't think I'd ever seen him look more troubled.

"I'm sorry, son," Mr. Freedman said to me. "I'm, well...sorry."

"What?" I asked.

"They broke the terms," Mr. Freedman replied. "These bastards broke the terms that had been brokered with the Priests."

"Huh?"

"What he means to say," the man in the blue tie said, "is that you're all targets now. You and your mother and Gemma. Unfortunately, they already got to your friends from the gym before we could react."

"But Nate-Neck and Klowner didn't know anything," I protested. "Those guys had no idea what was going on between my dad and the Priests. I purposefully kept them out of it."

No one answered. The message was clear. The Priests didn't give a fuck.

And to these agents, Nate-Neck and Klowner were nothing more than collateral damage, innocent cadavers left in a dirty alley that were just another part of the job.

But those guys were dead because of me, I thought. Dead because of me.

"The van, McCutcheon," the Marshal in the green tie said. "It's our opinion that it's your best option."

The guy with the blue tie looked at me with calm, cool, sure-of-himself eyes, as if he was about to nudge me nicely along down toward the bottom of the stairs. Suddenly and ferociously I seized him with a C-clamp throat grip, ready to yank his fucking windpipe out.

After that I'd spin, gouge his partner in the eyes, and fire off a groin shot that would send his nuts into his lungs.

"What the hell did you guys do?" I demanded.

The Marshal in the green tie quickly ripped a sidearm from his belt, jammed it into my back, and then stepped extra close so as not to cause a commotion with any of the surrounding students.

"Calm down, son," he whispered into my ear, not wanting to draw attention to himself, even though a few kids couldn't help but notice the unusual disturbance. "Let my partner go, and calm down."

He pressed the barrel of the weapon into my kidney with enough force to let me know in no uncertain terms that if he had to blow a hole through the bottom of my back in order to get me to release his partner from my vise grip, he would.

"Somebody better start talkin'," I said as I removed my hand from his partner's throat.

"None of this is about you, McCutcheon," the guy in the green tie said as the guy in blue struggled to catch his breath. "None of this is about Freedman. None of this is about your father. None of this is about your friends from the gym or your sister or your mother, either. The only person this is about is D'Marcus Rose."

"Who?" I asked.

"D'Marcus Rose," Mr. Freedman replied with a

defeated shake of his head. "The United States Government, courtesy of your father, just nailed themselves the High Priest."

"My father?" I said.

"After your fight he escaped," Mr. Freedman told me. "And turned snitch."

"The phrase we prefer to use is that he turned state's evidence," replied the man in the green tie. "The head of the snake is now in custody."

"And Demon's in custody, too, son," Mr. Freedman said as he put his hand on my shoulder seeking to put my mind at ease.

"Well, actually..." said the agent.

"You mean he's not?" Mr. Freedman asked, his eyebrows raised.

"You'll have to talk to Stanzer."

"I'm talking to you," Mr. Freedman replied with heat in his eyes.

"This Demon guy," the Marshal replied. "Put it this way, he's a whole different bowl of soup."

"And that means?"

"Hold on, hold on," I said. It took me a moment to get my hands wrapped around the whole thing. "What you're telling me is that the Priests now think I had something to do with the arrest of the High Priest and we're all being targeted for revenge? Is that what's going on here?"

"Our job is to serve the citizenry, son. We get an opportunity to take down a criminal of this significance, we owe it to the people of the community to do so."

"But where's that leave me?" I said. I turned to Mr. Freedman. "I thought there was a deal. I thought I was going to Radiance. I thought I was being given a second chance."

He couldn't even raise his eyes to look at me.

"It's a scale, McCutcheon," said the agent in green. "You put two things on a scale and then you see which carries more weight. In the business of stopping bad guys, you always take the one that carries the most weight."

I rubbed my forehead. "You think they know where we now live?" I asked.

The guy in green nodded.

"You think they know where my mom works?"

Again, I got a head nod. The guy in blue had stopped talking to me though, still clearly pissed that I had put him in a throat lock.

"You think they know . . ."

"Look, kid, we don't have all day," snapped the Marshal in the blue tie. "Your mother is in the van. Your sister is in the van. The question is, are you going to enter the van or not?"

"To go where?" I asked.

"Could be Jackson, Mississippi," said the guy in the green tie. "Could be Flagler, Florida. Could be Cedar Rapids, Iowa, or Bellevue, Washington, or even Vancouver British Columbia. We can't tell you that right now."

"And if you don't come, you'll never know," said the guy in the blue tie as if it were some kind of threat.

"You mean I'll never see Gem again?"

"Not even a goddamn postcard on your thirtieth birthday," he answered as he rubbed his neck. I could tell this fed wanted a piece of me. But fuck him, I thought. I'm right here if he wants some.

"What about my stuff?" I asked.

"You get new stuff."

"And what about..."

"McCutcheon! Hey, McCutcheon," came a voice from about forty yards away. "Sorry it took me so long."

I snapped my head around and saw Kaitlyn waving at me.

"Be right there, babe," she said holding up one finger. "Just gotta drop this in the main office."

Kaitlyn disappeared inside a door.

"Look, son, it's a simple question and we're officially out of time," said the agent in the green tie. "You enter the white van and we'll protect you. You stay here and give it a go on your own, there's not much we can do other than warn you that your life is in serious danger. What's it gonna be?"

"What about her?" I asked in reference to Kaitlyn. "Is she safe?"

"See that gardener across the way?" I looked across the lawn at a guy in a green jumpsuit trimming a hedge. "He's one of us. And we have two custodians on campus right now as well. We'll keep our eyes fixed on her for about a month or so, and by then we'll know for sure if additional steps need to be taken."

"But is she in danger?"

"We'll do our best to protect her."

"But is she in danger?" I asked again. After all, Willie the Weasel had seen us together not too long ago.

"You want odds?" I was asked.

"I want odds," I said.

"They're low," the Marshal in the green tie replied. "I'd say fifteen percent the Priests have her on their radar."

"Look, we're done here," said the guy in the blue tie, finally losing his cool. "The white van is a one-way street. Once you enter, it's a done deal. And if you don't enter now, it's also a done deal. There are no second chances, kid. What's it gonna be?"

I turned toward Mr. Freedman with a "What should I do?" look in my eyes. Again, his gaze dropped to the ground without offering me a reply. He'd been through Wit Sec. He'd told me so. And everything he seemed to be communicating to me right now by not saying a word about it seemed to tell me that it was the last place a person really wanted to go.

But when the leverage goes against you, sometimes a person has no choice.

It was a lose/lose situation, and I had about five seconds to make my final decision.

"McCutcheon. McCutcheon!" Kaitlyn called out as she popped out of the building. Her smile was warm and bright. "Sorry for the wait."

I lifted my gaze and looked over at Kaitlyn. We made eye contact from about twenty-five yards away. A tear formed in the corner of my eye, then rolled down my cheek.

A moment later I turned and scampered down the steps, hustling toward the van.

"McCutcheon! Hey, where're you going?"

"Don't look back, son," said the Marshal in the green tie as he held my arm by the elbow and escorted me toward the road. "Don't wave. Don't acknowledge her. We don't know who is watching and you don't want to put her in harm's way."

"McCutcheon. Hey!" Kaitlyn screamed. "McCutcheon!!"

"Whatever you do," I was told, "you can never look back."

The side door to the white van slid open and I ducked my head and hopped inside while Mr. Freedman wordlessly remained on the curb. I took a seat between my terrified sister and my crying mother, and a moment later the vehicle sped off.

And *poof!* I disappeared.